Waltzing
With
Tumbleweeds

Novels by Dusty Richards

Noble's Way
From Hell to Breakfast
By the Cut or Your Clothes
Servant of the Law
Lawless land
Ranchers Law
The Abilene trail
The Ft Smith Trail
Deuces Wild
Aces Wild
Queen of Spades
The Natural

http://www.dustyrichards.com

Waltzing
With
Tumbleweeds

Dusty Richards

AWOC.COM Publishing
Denton, Texas

Contents

Dedication

I dedicate this book to Peggy Fielding who has so generously helped so many writers—a lady who never knows how to say no to anyone. Gosh, she's been inspirational, encouraging, and mother like. "Now you do something with all these lovely stories." Shucks, Peg, this cowboy never figured they were lovely in the first place. I tip my Stetson to her and thank the good Lord he sent her to us.

— Dusty Richards

Introduction

Short stories are like rain in the desert. They come further apart now than before. Some days I am all involved in a book and this idea comes creeping in and I stay up past midnight to find out what is supposed to be on this paper.

Maybe like Michelangelo said about the stone. "I carve out what God left me inside the rock." So goes my writing. I print out what he left me on the paper.

Who knows what good and evil lurks in our subconscious, some larceny, some love, some violence, some kindness, some arson, some passion—the list is endless. Yet a story comes, no doubt from my volumes of research that are set chronologically in the days of the west.

Over the years, I have found the short fiction entertaining to reword and write, short epistles, no major commitment, most of them are intense, most have a message through the main character and the story line. Dusty's western pulps, you can call them. Peggy Fielding got to reading them and chewed me out for not doing more with them, but books have been my mainstay the past decade so the shorts have fallen into the computer cracks.

— Dusty Richards

Waltz to the Wind

The sharp March wind swept the yellow wild flowers and tossed them like a tempest sea. Standing before a window on the second story of Millie's House of Pleasure, she wrapped the silk duster more tightly around her body. Poor blossoms, so mistreated by the bitter forces, she felt pained for them.

Win-Anne had come to Dodge City in the cold of winter. Anxious to earn the easy money that others spoke of, she joined the girls at Millie's House. The days had begun to lengthen, but business remained slow.

Most of the cowboys were still in Texas gathering cattle. The new green grass would be headed and brown before the vast herds arrived. All the talk about riches was just that—talk.

Like the flowers, she had been tossed about with less than tenderness, and then some day she too would shrivel and die. There was no justice for her kind. Long ago, she had given up the notion of some gallant knight riding up and taking her away from this place or any other parlor house where she worked.

The Texas boys were mostly young, inept, but sweet. A few were snakes, cruel, deliberately defeating in their actions toward her. A shudder ran up her arms at the thought of such worthless wags. She closed her eyes and tried to shut out the past pain, like the flowers scattered across the fresh green carpet, she too had been bent, whipped and slapped.

Three abreast, she saw them come riding. They waved their hats in youthful excitement. Even tried to get their horses to buck and no doubt were laughing as they approached Dodge.

Would they stop at Millie's? Her heart quickened. Sometimes boys that age—her age—were too bashful and first visited the saloons for whiskey courage. She hurried down the stairs to be available. In anticipation, her breath caught in her throat when their boot heels clattered on the porch. Her heart quickened at the sound and no matter how hard she tried, there was no way she could turn down her smile.

Within minutes, she was in the arms of Earl. Belly to belly, they danced around the parlor to the piano player's tingling melody. His firm embrace drove away all her regrets. This was why she did what she did. His closeness, her knowing he wanted her, idolized her and even loved her for the moment. In this brief span of time, she was the flower out of the wind.

The Hawks Will Miss Him

A strong breath from the far away Gulf of Mexico tossed and curled the eternal waves of feathered bluestem. Across the endless rolling hills, ten million stalks of tall grass waltzed without a bride. He rested his sweat stained gray pony on the rise. Hat brim cupped in his hand, he mopped the wetness from his brow to his sleeve. High above him, a red tail hawk soared, challenged this invasion of his land. The bird's shrill threat drew a small smile on his dark brown lips.

Ready to go on, he booted the gray off the ridgeline. He pushed westward again. The face of the sun grew higher; he rode down a deep draw toward a paintless house and sheds clustered under some gnarled post oak trees. Here a dependable spring flowed out of the mottled marble limestone that underlaid the red cherty soil; he could recall its cool taste. Drawing closer, he watched her clothing dance on the line like puppets on strings.

She raised up from her wash board to make out the rider. With the brown eyes of a wary doe, she studied his approach. Soon Willy New Trees recognized him. If his appearance pleased or shocked her, the bland expression on her smooth, handsome face conveyed no emotion.

He dismounted heavily and then tried to restore the circulation in his numb lower limbs by stomping his run-over boots. Deliberate like, she stripped the suds and water from her forearms; swept the long dark hair from her face with the sides of her hands.

"I will put your horse away," she said and then she stood on her toes as if to check his back trail. Seeing nothing, she took the reins and led the gray toward the nearest shed.

He pulled the material of his pants away from the chafed skin on the insides of his legs. Then he adjusted his crotch for some comfort. With a shrug of his tight shoulders, he began to look around her place.

Hiding at the corner of the house, six coal black eyes peered at him. Suspicious and cautious, her young children soon drew back. He heard them snicker up their noses as if they knew this man's purpose for being there. Then the sounds of their bare feet running away carried to his ears. Willy returned from the shed. With a toss of her raven black hair, she led him around to the front door.

"Hungry?" she asked when they were inside. Not waiting for his reply, she began to stoke up the fire in her small cast iron stove. He pushed the hat back on his head, took a ladder back chair and seated himself. From his place, he could study her figure. No longer a girl, her fuller body suited him. She clanged the kettle bottoms placing them on the metal surface. Then she straightened like a willow tree as if satisfied they would heat without any more care.

Her thin soles shuffled on the gritty floor and she took a seat across the paint-chipped white table from him. She rested her olive brown arms on the yellow oil cloth; her ample breasts ready to spill out of the wash worn waist.

"How far behind are they?" she asked.

She meant Parker's marshals. They coursed this land of the Osage searching for him. To arrest him, to drag him in irons back to Ft Smith, where the red brick courthouse sat perched high on the Arkansas River bank, to force him to look into the fierce eyes of Judge Parker and then that devil-man would stretch his neck on the gallows for killing Charlie One-Dog.

"Maybe a day or two."

"Not much time?"

"Not much time."

She understood his predicament. Without a word, she rose to her feet and went to stand beside the iron poster bed. Her long fingers began to undo the buttons on her blouse, then her skirt.

She removed her clothing; next she climbed onto the mattress and pulled a feed sack sheet over her naked form. Above the whistle of the wind at the eves, he heard her clear her throat to summon him.

He rose, dropped his suspenders. For a long moment, he stared down at the glaring rectangle of sunlight on the floor, framed by the door way—with effort he walked over, closed it, shutting out the light. Then he undressed.

In bed with her, with care, his calloused hands molded her body. Her eyes began to dance with the pleasure that he caused her. She giggled softly when his fingertips probed her. At last, she nodded in readiness, rolled onto her back in a protest of springs, raised her knees and spread them apart.

Together they flew like birds of prey—soared as high as eagles. Swept over the land, two alone, joined as one forever. A sheet of sweat lubricated their bellies. The air grew thinner for both of them. Then they fell into an abyss and drowned.

Soon she arose, dressed and went to her stove. She dished out a heaping plate of white beans and cooked green squash, placed it on the table top, then wordless and not looking back, she slipped outside, quietly closing the door behind her.

He sat up, combed his black hair in his fingers. Bone weary, he redressed, then took a place at the table and ate her food. After he finished, he went outside to find her. She was washing on the rub board again.

"Must you go?" she asked, avoiding his eyes.

"Yes."

"Then I will get your horse." She dried her hands and forearms. Still not daring to look at him, she started for the shed. With her back turned, he slipped five silver dollars from his pocket into the tub of gray water. Then he went to meet her half way and took the reins from her.

"You are a good woman, Willy New Trees."

She nodded that she had heard him. They stood in awkward silence, each afraid to touch the other. Only the rush of the wind as their witness. At last, he mounted his pony and rode away.

While the sun traveled westward, his grey horse's chest parted the sea of blue stem like the bow of a ship. He rode without thoughts. His belly full, his groin at rest. From out of nowhere, a sharp blow struck his back. The force of the .44/40 bullet knocked him face down from his saddle before he ever heard the rifle's blast or the distant shouts of the men behind him.

Sprawled on the ground, the rich sweet aroma of the tall grass teased his nose, a smile crossed his drawn face, then the copper flavor of his own blood filled his mouth. Good. He would never have to face the devil-man Parker nor his gallows... A red tail hawk on high, heralded his death.

They Speak of Her Around Campfires

Sandal clad feet churned up loose sand in the dry wash. Out of wind, her lungs felt on fire. Fierce cramps stung both legs and a sharp catch in her side threatened to bowl her over. She held the many-layered skirts high enough to free her knees. Despite the discomfort, she ran on. With dread, she glanced back for signs of pursuit. Nothing. No need to try to conceal her footprints, her captors could track a lizard across bare rocks.

At last, she slowed her strides to a stilted walk approaching the forks in the watercourse and she looked both ways. A huge gnarled walnut grew on the alluvial plain; its shade tempted her to drop and rest. She dared not stop yet. With a shake of her head, she dismissed the notion and began to run again down the broad sparkling wash.

Hours before, she'd slipped away from the other women who were busy digging up Century plant roots to make *tiswain*—Apache whiskey. Using the excuse that her belly hurt, she went around some junipers. From her cover, she slipped away before they noticed her missing. This was her chance to escape. Sometimes they let an escapee get away. She hoped that would be her case and they would not track her down.

The poor Mexican girl, Margarita, they brought back and after that they tied her up every night. She soon lost her mind. Reduced to a mumbling incoherent thing, she roamed around the camp. A vision of the girl's sad mental state made Alberta's shoulders tremble as she ran.

How long had she been among the Chirichuas? Nine or ten months, she lost track of time. One day long ago, unaware, she had been hanging clothes on the line at the

ranch yard, the cotton ropes that her husband Charlie
Macon had strung for her. Next thing she knew, she was
jerked up and forced to lay belly down across his horse.
The screaming near naked buck pinned her painfully over
his lap and despite her struggles to get free, he galloped
away with her.

At first, she felt guilty for letting him abduct her. Was it
really her fault? How could she have avoided being
captured? She certainly never would have gone willingly.
Would Charlie accept her back as his wife—soiled as she
was? No matter—she looked at the spiny trees on both
sides of the watercourse and ran harder.

Her heart pounded under the thin material of her waist,
her tender breasts shook with her strides. She rounded the
corner and ran face to face into two dismounted Apaches.

An ear-shattering scream ripped from her throat. Both
men blinked in disbelief. Unable to run a step further, she
dropped to her knees and closed her eyes to await her fate.
Hands clasped together before her, she began to pray.

"Our father who art in heaven—"

"Miss! Miss!" someone shouted in her ear.

Alberta tried to shake free from the panic that gripped
her as if she had gone mad. Someone spoke to her,
someone spoke to her in English. Did those two Apaches
speak that fluent English? With her hand, she swept back
the long brown hair from her face. She blinked up at the tall
man in the sparkling blue uniform with gold buttons that
glinted in the sunlight. "You're a white woman, aren't
you?" he asked gently lifting her to her feet.

It must be hard to tell I'm white. "Yes," she said and
felt a wash of grateful relief sweep over her.

"Toby," the Lieutenant shouted to one of his scouts.
"Go get this lady a horse to ride."

"Alberta—Alberta Macon's my name." She
straightened, embarrassed by her impulsive urge to clutch

this man. Gathering her wits about her, she fought for composure. Hard to believe, but at last she was safe. She looked around at the junipers and pinons, no sight of anything. Then as the truth settled in on her, she closed her eyes and nodded gratefully. Her prayers had been answered.

"Jeff Liggett. Lieutenant U.S. Cavalry."

"Nice to meet you, Lieutenant."

"Your husband?"

"He's at the ranch near the base of the Whetstone Mountains. Charlie Macon's his name."

"Yes, I saw your name on a report some time ago. I'm sure he'll be glad you're alive."

"Yes," she said, but without enthusiasm.

"I'll take you back to Ft. Bowie and we can send him word that you're safe."

Alive, yes, but not unsoiled. She took both her hands and swept her long hair back.

"I have a leather thong if you would like to tie it?" He offered it to her.

"Yes, thank you." That way her hair would be out of her face on the ride to the fort. She accepted his generous offer and tied it back.

"Can you walk up this bank?" he asked.

"I could walk to hell with you," she said then realized her words and blushed.

"Only to the horses, ma'am."

"Yes."

The patrol was composed of a dozen enlisted troopers, four Apache scouts and the lieutenant. They arrived at Ft. Bowie at sundown. Final rays of sunshine bathed Signal Peak that rose above the camp.

They halted at the orderly's post. The adobe hut fit in the U-shaped arrangement of buildings that composed the fort's various structures including some nice bungalows, no doubt for the officers and their wives. Ft. Bowie nestled in a wide pass between the mountains. Brushy junipers clung to the hillsides above them.

Several passing soldiers stared at her. Obviously her squaw clothing made them take a second look.

"I'll arrange a place for you to stay," the lieutenant said.

"Thank you," she said and began to dismount.

Her weak sea-legs shocked her when she stepped down light headed. The world began to tilt. Her knees threatened to buckle. Next, her vision blurred. She lost her grasp on the army saddle, and she fainted.

"Everyone clear out!" An authoritative woman's voice ordered. "Out! Out! The poor girl needs some rest."

Alberta raised her head up. She found herself lying on a clean smelling bed that made her sweaty-campfire smoke flavored body stink like some kind of an animal.

"Get some rest now, dear," the gray haired woman said.

"But I'm so filthy," she protested.

"You're too tired to do a thing about it right now. Rest. We can wash those sheets later."

"My name is—"

"Alberta Macon, the lieutenant told me that already."

The short woman in the starched blue dress smiled at her. "Georgia Kline is my name. My husband Abner's the post sutler. Now go to sleep and stop worrying, they've already sent for your husband."

"Oh," she said and laid back on the pillow to stare at the tin ceiling tiles. Why did she fear the notion of Charlie Macon coming for her? Sooner or later she had to expect to be returned to her "man." What would he think? She squeezed her eyes shut and soon fell into a deep slumber.

When Alberta awoke, Georgia proved her mettle as a hostess. The woman had a large copper bathtub full of hot water and perfumed soap ready. Her first real bath in almost a year. A long handled brush proved a great tool as she sought to erase every trace of Apache from her skin. Her bath water had turned lukewarm when at last she stepped out to dry herself with the Turkish towel.

For a long moment she stared in shock at the thin woman in the tall, oval mirror. She had lost many pounds, her legs looked like sticks, her stomach drawn in and her once globe shaped breasts shrunk to pears. With her hands, she swept her long hair back from her face, still peering at the reflection of this stranger in the looking glass. Would Macon even know her?

"We'll shampoo your hair with yucca soap and then braid it," Georgia said, helping her into a robe.

"How will I ever repay you?"

"We won't worry about that."

"Oh, but I must." She leaned closer to the mirror and examined her face. "He won't even know me." She ran her hand over her deep, sunburned cheek. "My skin's dark as a squaw. Oh Georgia, I should never have come back."

"Nonsense, you belong with your own people, with your husband." Georgia guided her away from the mirror. "We need to wash your hair now. Why, your husband will bust his buttons when he sees you. Pretty girl and all like you are. Why he'd be foolish to do anything else."

"No, he won't. I'm soiled."

"Here, here, let's look to the bright side of things, my dear."

Alberta shook her head in defeat. In her heart, she knew nothing would ever break through his stubbornness. He would never accept her.

With a deep breath for strength, she bent her head over the washbasin. If only she could scrub away those nights she laid under his muscle-corded belly. The many times he made her forget she was in a grass thatched wickiup, making love with a man who wasn't her husband. Feeling all the things, she had never felt before. All those crazy intimate nights with her crying out in wanton pleasure, something she had never ever done in bed with Macon.

Her regrets consumed her until she no longer could face the people on the base. She could not stand them staring at her, knowing she had laid with an Apache. Been penetrated by a savage... allowed him access. She had not fought enough, she had succumbed too easily... submitted willingly. Filled with dread of what the future would bring, she closed her eyes, but even they denied her tears.

She kept her lids tightly shut. Her shoulder quaked under Georgia's comforting hand. Any day—any time Macon would come for her. Or even worse he would ignore the message. What would she do then?

Two more long days crawled by. After an embarrassing physical examination, the post physician declared, she was likely not pregnant and apparently free of venereal disease. He muttered before he left, she was very lucky.

Meanwhile Georgia sheltered her from the others. Alberta could hear the various visitors in the other room.

"Oh, she is not up to having company today?"

"Did she take an Apache husband?"

"I don't know," Georgia would say. "She never told me."

Alberta's memory could recall every illicit, intimate moment she spent with him. It branded her brain like a hot iron scorched a calf's skin at a roundup. The bitter smoke of the burning hair even hurt her nostrils as she recalled it.

On Friday, Charlie Macon drove up in a buckboard. He wore a tie and his brown Sunday suit. She always called it his Sunday suit, though he never attended church. He wore it to town when he took out loans and he wore it to funerals. This time he wore it to pick up his errant wife.

Georgia fixed her a satchel complete with a cotton night shift, under garments, an everyday calico dress they sewed together. She wore a black skirt and a starched white blouse under a shawl for the ride home. No need for a hat, she couldn't get any darker than she already was. The soft slippers on her feet were hand-me-downs from another woman at the base.

"Afternoon," Macon said removing his wide brimmed Stetson for Georgia. His snow-white forehead contrasted with his deep leather colored face.

The two women looked at each other. Alberta rolled her lower lips under her sharp upper teeth. It would be hard to leave this true friend. Sadness stabbed her, she would never again have anyone to lean on like Georgia.

"Ready?" Macon asked, taking her bag.

"Yes."

"We better go. We've lots of miles," he spoke with his back to her as he loaded it in the rig.

"Good bye Georgia and thanks for everything."

"Good bye and God be with you my dear."

I'll need him. She waved and hurried to where he stood waiting to help her up in the buckboard.

Apache Pass behind them, the rusty red Dragoon Mountains lie ahead. She sat the spring seat beside her silent husband, touching his shoulder with hers on the bumps. Like sitting with a statue, an unmoved man in a thin veil of dust from the hooves of the trotting team.

The brown grassland of the Sulphur Valley spilled out around them. By sundown, they had passed through several small canyon mining towns. He stopped in Gleason. Without a word, he tied off the reins and went inside the store. In a few minutes, he returned with a sack of crackers, cheese and two cans of sardines and handed them to her with a, "Here."

Macon undid the lines and drove out of Gleason. A mile south, he pulled off the road into a dry wash, and speculated in silence over the fiery sunset far off over the Whetstones.

"We can camp here." He never looked at her, climbed down and began to unhitch the team.

Obviously he intended for them to dine on the food in the poke. For a long moment, she considered it then she climbed down and went off to relieve herself. When she came back, she set the food out on the tailgate.

He was busy hobbling the horses. There had been enough water in the pot hole to quench the animals' thirst. Two burlap wrapped jugs in the wagon bed contained their drinking water. She sipped some. Living so long on the move with Chirichuas, she had taught herself to temper her thirst. Macon joined her with a nod and began to eat.

Darkness set in on the hills around them. Finished eating, he hoisted the bedroll out and undid the straps. She tried to ignore the deepening light. The Gambell quail grew silent. A lone coyote threw his head back and howled until the stars began to twinkle.

"You coming to bed?" he finally asked.

She whispered, "yes," then swallowed a hard knot of dread. The time had come to be his wife again. What did she fear the most? Rejection? Accusation that she had not resisted? Or his damn smug silence? She had resisted.

The next few minutes in the bedroll beside him were the longest in her life. She dared not upset him, give him any clue of her life with the savage; she was his wife. Grateful he only lasted for a short while on top of her, then he rolled off and with his back to her, went to sleep.

His fluids seeped from her and she didn't bother to stem it. Her sore eyes stared at the stars. Like the lonely coyote, sleep eluded her. With only the galaxies to keep her company, she lay on her back, blankets to her chin and considered the future.

At sunup they shared a wordless breakfast of dry cheese and crackers. The food crumbled in her mouth. He hitched the horses. They drove through Tombstone as the sleepy-eyed miners in their dust floured clothing headed for their shift at the mines. Like the workers, she was headed for a cavernous existence; only there would be no small jokes, laughter or even words in hers. Macon would never forgive her.

Even during her captivity she had dreaded her return. Lying at night beside the savage, she had worried about how Macon would treat her. Now she knew. Deep inside, she rolled the notion over and over in her mind as they struck the road westward toward the Whetstones. Shunned was the word.

Things that needed to be done began to occupy her thoughts as they crossed the rolling, grassy plateau. She would clean the house. It would be spotless. Make a few new quilts, repair his clothes, there would be enough to occupy her time. Maybe not enough to stop her mind from plowing it up again and again. Work would satisfy her, she promised herself.

Sight of the clapboard house in late afternoon warmed her. He reined up at the corral, dismounted as if she wasn't even along. Macon never talked much before, but his silence had grown deeper. He was punishing her for her transgressions. She must do penance. Perhaps in time he would accept her again and fall into talking about his cows and horses, as he had formerly, including her in his few words.

Days went by. The nights were long beside his sleeping form. Since that first evening on the road near Gleason he had even ignored her body. Staring at the dark abyss of the open ceiling overhead, she wondered if her whole life would pass in this fashion. Ostracized in her own house, she closed her eyes, unable to even cry.

Macon left at daybreak that morning to check on a water hole. He took a small spade with him. All she could imagine he needed a shovel for; he never said. She had tossed the small rug over the line and was beating it with a bat size stick. The fury of her attack sent clouds of dust off in the wind.

Out of breath, she dropped the club and bent over to recover. A sobering notion washed over her; someone was watching her. Straightening up, warily, she turned to look around.

He squatted on the heels of his knee high boots. The tail of the white breechcloth hung down as he sat motionless. His black bangs needed to be trimmed, but his eyes told her he had not come for revenge.

"That is your enemy?" he asked as if mildly amused.

His words forced a smile on her face. How long since she had smiled?

"It has many ghosts in it," she said.

"You are happy here?" He tossed his head toward the house.

"Are you happy?" she asked sharply, not daring to answer him.

He dropped his gaze and shook his head. "No."

"I cannot live on the run all the time from the Army—"

"We could go to the White Mountains."

"Where is that?"

"Pines, cool streams. Many deer to eat."

"Would the soldiers search for us there?"

"No. It is a reservation."

"Would you be happy there?" She swept up the stick and watched him closely for his reaction to her question.

"Only if you would be with me."

She tapped her bat in the dirt. For a long moment, she studied the dusty toes of her slippers. How could she even consider doing this? A married woman run off with a savage? She must be mad even to consider the notion. Go live in some wild mountains, cook over a fire, do without a bed, a roof?

With a fling, she threw the stick aside and went to him. He rose and they melded into each other's arms.

"We may never have children."

His forehead pressed to hers. The great brown pupils looked into her very soul.

"We will have each other," he said and melted her heart.

"Yes, Nah-tice, we will have each other. I will get a horse," she said and started to turn away.

"No, I brought one for you."

She brightened at the prospect of a mate who knew she existed. Excited with her new-found decision and going away with him, she watched him run off into the greasewood. Two mounted Apache men she recognized returned with him. They put five horses in the corral. The pair laughed and grinned with each other.

"Why do they do that?" she asked him with a frown.

"To pay for you," he said and handed her the reins to a fine pony. She agreed with a nod. Macon wouldn't have to talk to those horses. Pleased with his trade, she quickly kissed him on the mouth to seal their arrangement and then mounted up. He smiled in approval at her actions and they rode away.

Four years later, Captain Jeff Liggett, the new military commander of Fort Apache stood on the porch of the post's headquarters in the early morning light. Alberta nodded to herself, noting his sparkling uniform. Drawing closer to him, she spoke in Apache for her two small children to stay close.

"Mrs. Macon, is that you?" he asked in disbelief.

"No, I am Alberta, wife of Nah-tice." She shook her head and then gathered the hair back from her face. "I am here to complain for my people."

"Complain?"

"Yes. There is a soldier by the name of O'Day that abused a young Apache girl two days ago. She is not a whore and this man used her."

"I will put that on report." He drew his shoulders up square and looked very official.

"I hope you do more than the last commander we had here. He did little about such bad things. There is more."

"More?" He frowned.

"Yes, last month, the beef they sent us was too tough to eat. I saved this jaw bone from one of them." She drew it from her pocket and shoved the polished bone at the man. "See he had even lost his teeth. So old and stringy you couldn't even make shoes from his meat."

"I understand, Mrs. Macon. There have been many things wrong here and I will correct them."

"I am Alberta, wife of Nah-tice."

"Yes, Alberta," he corrected himself. "I will see to these things at once."

She turned and shared a look at the knot of Apache men standing back at a respectable distance, listening to her complaining. She spoke to them in their tongue.

"I know this man. He is an honorable man and will be fair to us. I have told him our worst troubles."

They nodded they heard her. Satisfied, they turned and went about their business. With that completed, she called to her children swinging on the hitch rail to go with her. Of course, he would see to them, she knew this man well.

Appeared in the March 1991 Darlington Times,
Darlington, Md.

Heroes Were Never Born

They were buffalo hunters. And they were out of work because the slaughter of the southern herd was over. A handful of grizzly, unbathed buckskinners that lounged around Rosarita's cantina across the New Mexico line. Four men who lazed around, drinking bad whiskey, whiling away the money left from the final sales of hides and lamenting the end of a way of life.

"All the buffaloes are gone," Mulky Nelson said aloud with choking emotions rising in his normally tough voice. Earlier that morning, he had considered biting down on the .50-70 caliber Sharps hexagon muzzle and using his toe on the trigger to end his misery.

Whatever would he do? For a decade, he had hunted the wooly devils. Flush from the sale of robes, he always spent his earnings on voluptuous doves, cards and good whiskey. He didn't miss the overindulgence in pleasure as much as the exhilaration of squinting down his gun sights, squeezing off the trigger and seeing the shaggy beast fall dead.

At the end of each day, his ears rang from the muzzle blasts, his shoulder was tender from the powerful recoil and both his arms ached from helping the skinners peel off the hides. The copper musk of butchering in his nose, his fingers stiff from drying blood, Mulky ate handfuls of raw liver to restore his manhood. Even the buzzards, too full to fly, appreciated him. Damn. Those days were gone forever.

Mulky hated to see men like Measles Hankins, Big Dee Thompson and Ike Woolford sitting around in sullen depression. They deserved an ending better than that.

For a moment, he considered going the fifty yards to see Estelle, the settlement's only lully-tropping-woman, but the notion soon passed, having little appeal to him.

"Tell me something," he said, beckoning to Rosarita, the thick-bodied saloon owner.

"Yes?" she asked. looking standoffish across the bar.

"Are they all dead?" he asked, realizing the liquor was twisting his tongue.

"Yes."

"Good, I didn't want one of them left out there."

"When will you quit asking me?" she demanded. "Every last gawdamn buffalo is dead."

"I heard you," he said growing angry. The least, the woman with the fine black hair on her upper lip could say, was, 'Maybe there is one more left.'

He turned and mildly studied a new customer coming in the door: a lanky cowboy with jingling spurs, a fresh kerchief around his throat and a washed, clean shaven face.

Mulky heard him order a rye. Ha, he thought, that fat woman gets all her whisky from the same barrel of swill.

"You guys are hunters, ain't ye?" he asked them in his deep Texas drawl.

No one bothered to answer the hardly more than a boy. It was bad enough to have salt in a festering wound, no one needed to rub it in.

"Well," the cocky stranger swelled out his small chest, "I seen an old cow buffalo a week ago that you missed."

Four sets of marksmen-quality eyes glared at the cowboy. The scrape of chair legs on the dirt floor was noisy as the hunters stood up. Was the man lying—they searched each other's faces.

Measles beat the others to the man by seconds. He grabbed a fistful of the cowboy's shirt in one hand, the sharp honed skinning knife laid on the speaker's throat as the hider bent him backwards over the bar.

"You're fixing to be a dead liar," Measles said, through his rotting teeth.

"Wait!" Ike ordered, wrestling the knife arm back. Mulky helped him pull their irate companion off the ranch hand.

Freed, the shaken cowboy felt his throat to be certain the jugular vein was not severed. Pale faced and shocked, he looked wide eyed at them.

"I ain't lying," he began, holding his hand out to hold them off. "I was checking cattle a week ago down by the Frances Mountains. I saw her all right. She was a skinny cow, but when she saw me she high tailed it."

"Which way did she go?"

"West," he said, warily searching their faces.

"If you're a lying to us—" Measles started for him, but Mulky and Ike blocked his way.

"Why would he lie?" Ike asked. "He knows we'll blow his head off if we don't find her."

"Yeah," Measles relented, sheathing his knife.

"I swear I seen her," the pale faced cowboy said. "She's an old cow."

"I sort of thought there ought to be one left out there," Mulky said, encouraged by the report. "A stray smarter than the rest. Damn, of the millions of them, one had to have enough brains to get away."

Measles laughed, scoffing, "They were all dumb."

"Listen to Mulky," Big Dee said, leaning on his gun barrel. "He may be right."

"Then let's go get her," Measles said.

"Wait, let's have a contest," Ike said. "Each man goes on his own after her. The one brings her down wins the pot."

"What pot?" Measles asked.

"Money that we put up," Mulky said, impatient with the red-specked-faced, dull-witted member of the bunch.

"How much money?"

"Well, Ike?" Mulky turned to their educated member for a plan.

"Two hundred and fifty apiece. That's a thousand in the pot for the man gets her." Ike had a dreamy way of acting when his brain was working that made Mulky jealous of his skills. No one, not even the trickiest hide buyer, ever outwitted Ike.

"What's the rules?" Mulky asked, expecting their educated cohort to do it right. He was not disappointed when Ike pushed his floppy brimmed hat back.

"No one leaves here to hunt for her until sunup. Each man can take his skinning help along. But it's got to be a fair kill."

"What's fair mean?" Measles demanded.

"Ike means running her off a bluff doesn't count for killing her," Mulky said,

"Yeah, that's a good rule." Measles agreed.

The money was put up. They drank two rounds, but each one was too superstitious to discuss out loud the existence of one more buffalo. Mulky could feel the tension build among the men as his own stomach roiled at the prospect of a last hunt.

As he stepped outside the cantina, Mulky rubbed his sweaty palms on his britches. Inside his chest, his heart beat so fast, he could hear his blood gurgling. No woman had ever done that much to him.

"Where are you headed?" Measles shouted after him.

"To hire a skinner."

"Yeah, you're heading out," the man accused.

"It's a good two days ride to those mountains," Mulky said, aggravated by the challenge of his sportsmanship. "I'll be here at sunup. See that you're here."

"You better be," Measles warned.

Mulky knew he must ride fast to find his helper. Blue was a cross-eyed Comanche that could track a tit mouse over bare rocks. He intended to hire the tracker as his skinner.

Two hours later, he disgustedly found the old man passed out on the ground thirty feet from the brush arbor where his wife Red Bird sat sewing. When he rode up, she never looked up from her stitchery.

"Is Blue drunk?" he asked.

"He's always drunk," she said noncommittal as Mulky dismounted.

"Well, I need him to track down a buffalo."

Red Bird looked up. "You drunk too?"

"No, there's one left. A cowboy saw her last week down near the Frances Mountains."

"Was he drunk?"

"No," Mulky said amused at her stubbornness. "I think one still lives."

"What you want Blue for?"

"To track it down for me."

"His brain is too whiskey soft. He never find it."

"I brought plenty of coffee." he said handing her the pouch. "There's a thousand bucks riding on who ever finds her."

"You bet that much?" she asked.

"Two-fifty is all I bet. But I want to win it."

Red Bird nodded in understanding. "We make him sober."

But sobering Blue was a tougher job than Mulky imagined. It was past midnight before they returned to

Rosarita's. He did not want Red Bird to come along, but decided in the end she might help him keep Blue sober.

Mulky hurried around getting up his mules and loading panniers on their backs. He hated the gyp-tasting water from Rosarita's well, but there was no time to go elsewhere to fill his kegs.

The short Comanche looked hung over in the campfire's light when Mulky shook him to awareness. Quickly, Mulky turned away and averted his gaze. He could never stand to look straight at the cross-eyed buck.

"Why did you bring me here? What do you want?" Blue grumbled.

"I told you ten times last night. For you to track down the last one for me."

"Track what?"

Mulky threw his hat down and nearly stomped on it. This whiskey-soaked devil had used up his last thread of patience.

"Blue," he began tersely, "in a half an hour, we're going to ride the winds for the Frances Mountains and you better find her for me."

Blue shook his head. "No more buffalo."

"One left and we're going to find her," Mulky vowed.

"Eat. Be light soon and time to go." Red Bird interrupted their argument by shoving each of them a tin plate of hot cakes sweetened with sorghum.

At sunup, Mulky warily studied his field of opponents. Measles had hired a skinny boy mounted on a ewe-necked bay. Ike's helper was a Mexican that lived nearby. The Latin rode an unspirited Indian pony. Big Dee sat on his bay with his legs bunched up because the stirrups were too short. The man's Kiowa wife was mounted on a nervous colt. Mulky considered the giant's chances of finding the buffalo as less than the others. But blind luck was not to be overlooked, even for the slow moving big man and Mulky knew such people had found greater fortunes without skill.

A stiff wind was whipping up dust when Ike fired off his pistol and the contest began. The "hee-yaws" and the thunder of hooves revealed a real horse race as they left out.

But in a half hour, Mulky pulled up his pony, satisfied he would shortly kill him. He settled for a jog. Besides Blue and Red Bird, who led the pack mules were a full mile behind. Wryly, he considered his outfit scattered worse than a widow woman's children.

Mulky had lost track of the others too. Nothing out there, but a vast alkali flat stretching for miles and miles. The tufts of stunted grass were chalk-coated with nary a tree anywhere.

"Dead Wolf Springs," Blue announced when he rode up. "I had a vision."

Somehow, Mulky did not trust the alcoholic Indian's capacity for fortune telling. Blue's brain had, for too long, been pickled in post rot gut. He did wonder though if the man's daydream had even a hint of accuracy.

"How far away are these springs?" he finally asked.

"Long ways."

"There's no sense killing our horses," Mulky said, worried the others had already found and shot her. If they hadn't, he doubted pressing their horseflesh any harder would gain any advantage.

The third day, the little barren hills were close enough to touch. There was no sign of the others as he waited while Blue dismounted and checked a game trail leading into the range.

"See any tracks?" he asked, irritated at their lack of luck finding even a trace so far.

The Comanche nodded with a scowl of disbelief on his wrinkled burnt leather face.

"One has been here," Blue announced.

"You mean a plain old Texas range cow."

"No!" The man appeared shaken by his discovery. "This was made by a she buffalo."

The words slapped Mulky. The cowboy had not lied. No one drunk or sober could out track that cock-eyed Blue. A ripple of excitement charged through Mulkey's saddle weary body. He rubbed his sweaty palms on his dust coated britches. Even his dry mouth flooded with saliva. *There was a survivor.*

If they could only find it before the others.

Blue started off on foot toward the mouth of the canyon. Mulky caught the Injun's horse to lead it for him. Then he checked on Red Bird and the pack train's progress. She was a half mile behind. Satisfied she would follow them, he booted his horse after the tracker.

The barren rock walls rose above him; the canyon floor was flooded with a narrow dry wash. Without the wind, the chasm heated oven like, he urged his pony after Blue who disappeared around a bend.

When Mulky came around the corner, he nearly swore. A box canyon enclosed them and there was no buffalo. Damn. Where had she gone?

"She went up there." Blue pointed up the towering sheer face of the cliff.

"How? What's she got wings?" he demanded as he squinted skeptically at the dazzling height.

"Small trail." Blue indicated the shelf on the wall.

"You're saying a buffalo cow went up that?" Mulky asked in disbelief as he dismounted.

Blue nodded. "Maybe ghost huh?"

"There ain't any way," Mulky said, feeling defeated as well as awed by the escape route. He noticed Blue had sat down between two dried dead scrub bushes.

"What's wrong with you?" he demanded.

"Blue, no like ghosts."

"There ain't no such things."

"Blue, no go over the mountain."

"What would you like?" he asked, reaching for the butt of his Navy Colt. "To go over there or die here?"

"Better to die here than get mixed up with spirit."

He could see the old man was dead set on balking. That was a problem with Indians that Mulky understood, they hated ghostly things.

"Just wait here then," he said, going for the Sharps in the scabbard. "She ain't no ghost."

"How you know?"

"Trust me. I ain't afraid," Mulky said. Besides nothing would dissuade him. Only a living animal left tracks. This one was a buffalo, the last of its kind and worth a thousand dollars. Mulky Nelson the last buffalo hunter. Why this hunt would make headlines in the New York newspapers.

There was no telling, he might go on stage and tell city folks how he tracked down the lone survivor. People made money doing worse things than that. Besides it would beat sitting around Rosarita's and her lamenting along with the other stinking buffalo hunters. He could almost hear the theater goers applause as he struck the trail.

The climb was steep. His heavy .50 caliber rifle did not make hugging the wall any easier. Soon the horses and Blue were mere specks below him. Atop the first ridge, he rested and studied the jumbled range. No sign of his prey. He pressed on along the mountain's spine. Then he spotted the cloven track in a soft place where the wind had deposited fine dust. His heart began to pound. Heady with his discovery, he trod the narrow hogback with a thousand foot drop off either side.

He stopped at a sheer drop off. Had the cow gone over this edge and fallen to her death, depriving him of his treasure? This would be his lot. Full of dread, he leaned over the edge. Then something on the canyon floor caught his eye.

A skinny buffalo cow stood in the shade of a dwarfed cottonwood. Chewing her cud, she shook her shaggy head at gnats and flicked her short tail from time to time.

The very last one, her ribs showed through her thin hide as he lifted the stock of the Sharps to his shoulder. She was not with calf, probably too old to breed. The end of a race represented by an emaciated specimen.

He clicked up the rear sight and took aim, his finger on the trigger ready to squeeze off 400 grains of black powder. He hesitated. There was something in his eye. Was he going blind? What was blurring his vision?

A tear wet his cheek and another fell as he lowered the gun barrel. Let someone else shoot her. He turned and started to leave unable to swallow the knot behind his tongue.

The others would never bother to look up there, since he had come out empty handed. Maybe she would live a while longer. A few bottles of whiskey would silence Blue and some material for new dresses would hush Red Bird's words about the matter.

As he picked his way down the mountain, he regretted one thing—the theater and his telling audiences how he shot the last southern herd buffalo. A smile crossed his lips. Maybe he could do that anyway. How in the hell would they know he hadn't pulled the trigger?

This won Fiction writer of the Year award in 1988 from "Tales of the Old West" magazine

A Sioux Widow's Lament

The wind would erase the tears and the wails of the Sioux warrior's widow who had lost her man in battle. The young brave had ridden with Chief Gall from the camp of the Sioux and the Cheyenne to meet the long Knives. She remembered his red and white pony chesting the water of the Big Horn River as he went to war. His lance high, bow slipped over his head, his war cries mixed with the others anxious to meet with the enemy.

The yellow haired, buckskin-clad leader called Custer came to make war on her people. Into the valley of the Bighorn, the Seventh Cavalry had charged to meet a far superior force. Crazy Horse had swept in from the west; her brave husband with Chief Gall's forces had cut off their flank.

A hot June sun blazed on the hillside where over two hundred "blue pants" had died from arrow, bullets and lance. When the fiery sun set beyond the saw-toothed Bighorns, the woman shared no victory dance because her man had joined his brave ancestors who went before him.

The valley of the Bighorn was silent at the next dawn except for the drone of the flies and magpies. A thundershower would soon dampen the blood soaked ground and the grass, nourished by bones of dead bison, would hide all the scars. The blades of grass would wave in the brilliant sunshine and whisper nothing of the infant who had been held to a warm breast and not allowed to cry as his people died nearby.

It was time to go to another place. There were too many to feed, the chiefs said. Winter would blow cold; the people would need to dry much buffalo to sustain themselves through the harsh weather. The dead had to be deserted. But, the people left the bodies on high platforms for the gods to claim.

There was no time for rest now. The widow piled her goods on her man's warhorse. The travois tracks would soon be erased by the wind as her people moved towards the north.

From this day forth, the brave people's lives would be as bitter as the green bile that ruined a buffalo's liver. The white man had killed the people's shaggy, kindred brother, then left the sustenance of the Sioux for the coyote and the fat magpie. No longer did millions of them thunder across the plains as they had in the woman's childhood.

The widow must face life without her man. She must secure a haven for her small son.

Head down, her breast full of sorrow, her moccasin steps would be heavy. She never looked back at the platform which bore her deceased husband. She would have more important things to concern her, the seed of her husband's loin who sat on the burdened warhorse. Ignorant of the harsh truth, the child would have to wait years to learn the grim facts. Then his people would be on reservations, their pride mere dust at the white man's feet. The man child would know the treachery of the Seventh at Wounded Knee and learn of the demise of Sitting Bull.

Ghost dancers could not save the woman's people. And in her final days, the woman's own heart and spirit would be broken. Her worn teeth would no longer be able to gnaw on the tough government issued beef; only the broth would sustain her in the last moons.

She would dream of the buffalo's taste to draw her saliva, but only the bitter gall flavor would be on her tongue as it had been since she had trudged out of the valley of the Little Bighorn. So it would be, until the spirits called her to the final resting place.

The Time He Rode

The Dodge Brothers touring car spluttered on the steep grade. Half sick with fear that the engine might die, Craft threaded the accelerator with his boot sole. To his relief, the motor overcame the cough and the rear tires dug in the soft sandy tracks, chugging powerfully to the top of the rise.

His major concern was the tall thin man in the passenger seat, Craft glanced aside to check on him. The ivory mustache was yellow at the corners. His thick eyebrows were snow white and hooded his steel blue eyes that stared straight ahead at the brown grass country that rolled off to south Texas. Deputy sheriff Bill Purdy, the famous ex-ranger, had not broken the past five miles of silence, not a word since sixteen year old Craft had driven him out of town.

"You herd this noisy thing around much?" Purdy finally asked.

"Quite a bit." Craft swallowed hard hoping he had given his important rider a good enough answer.

Purdy scowled in disapproval. "A man could go crazy listening to this infernal thing cluck."

"I'd have to agree a horse would be a lot more quiet."

"That's for sure. Why this thing spooks all the game clear out of the country. Did you see that doe run off back there?"

"Yes sir." It would be hard for him to impress the old man in any way about the autocar and its features.

"Those damn rustlers will hear us coming ten miles off," Purdy scoffed.

"Maybe they won't suspect a lawman coming in a car," Craft said as he fought the steering wheel to follow the wagon tracks.

"That's the only way it will work."

"Sir? Do you think they'll fight their way out?"

Purdy shook his head as if the matter was of little concern to him. Then he leaned forward and squinted out the sun blasted windshield at the country ahead.

"Did you ever know John Wesley Hardin?"

"Yes."

"Was he the killer they say he was?"

"I guess so. They say he once shot a man who snored too loud."

"Really?"

"Aw, old men spin lots of windy yarns, don't believe half the stuff they tell you. How old are you?"

"Sixteen."

"Hmm, when I was sixteen, I made my first trail drive to Kansas."

"Was it exciting?"

"Every dang bit as exciting as driving this car is for you."

Craft nodded in agreement as he wiped his sweaty left palm on his pants leg for the sixth time. Finally the old man was talking about something interesting.

"What did you do on the drive?"

"Cook's helper, till the night wrangler drowned crossing the Red River. Got a promotion after that, took care of the remuda."

"Were there Injuns?"

"There was everything on those drives to contend with: Injuns, herd cutters, plain rustlers and nesters."

"I've heard them cow towns were really wild?" Craft wondered about his carousing with wild women and exciting things that the man would admit to.

"Yes, they were straight from the pages of Hell."

The Dodge rumbled over some washboard places tossing both driver and passenger around. With only a small scrape of the metal to metal, he quickly found another gear to slow them down.

"This thing is sure rough riding," Purdy complained.

"It'll be smoother ahead." Craft pointed to where the ground became sandy again.

"Can't come soon enough." Purdy adjusted the snowy Boss of the Plains hat on his head and sat straight back on the seat.

"They say in a few years these cars will replace horses and wagons for travel."

"Heard the same silly thing about bicycles thirty years ago and they ain't done it yet. Hmm, they said we won't need horses after they invented them either."

Craft wished he'd never mentioned the part about autocars taking the place of horses; it had only made the old man sull up. He would have enjoyed hearing more about the cattle drive business and cow towns. Despite his gruffness, the slender six-foot officer didn't look stout enough to handle real tough lawbreakers. He hoped the man's reputation held when they found the suspects he sought.

A hiss of air came like a gunshot and Craft sunk behind the wheel as if he'd been hit. A flat tire—

Purdy frowned at him as he braked to a stop. "What's wrong with this contraption now?"

"Flat tire, sir."

Purdy studied the sky for the time and then looked pained at the inconvenience. "How long will it take you to fix it?"

"I'm not certain, I don't carry a watch."

Purdy removed the fancy engraved time piece on the gold chain from his vest, popped it opened and showed the face to Craft. Two-thirty. With a nod that he'd read it, he hurried out of the seat.

"It won't take but a jiffy," Craft promised and went back to the trunk, a high steamer like case on the rear of the car.

The rear axle finally jacked up, he sweated profusely as he pried the casing off the rim. Then, upset with the delay, he furiously inflated the a inner tube to locate the puncture, while the man Purdy seated himself on the running board, rolled cigarettes and acted like any malfunction was not his doing.

Twenty minutes later, the smell of gunpowder strong in his nostril from vulcanizing on the patch, Craft cranked the Dodge's engine to life. An hour later with a funnel of dust in their wake, they drove up to Oakley's Bar Seventy-Nine headquarters.

"You let me handle this," Purdy said as the brakes gritted to a stop. "Stay in the car, no matter what happens."

Craft nodded, letting the engine idle as Purdy unfolded himself out of the front seat. Deliberate like he reset the Stetson and then walked toward the house. A yellow dog who'd barked his head off since they'd arrived, ran off yelping at his approach.

Two men came out on the porch; they never smiled. Craft drew a deep breath, frozen to his seat, and spellbound, he watched things unfold. The Oakley brothers, Harp and Doan, were by reputation tough men, half Purdy's age too. Would they resist the old lawman and what should he do? Angry voices carried to him. Craft reached for the door latch—perhaps he should back Purdy's play. What could one old man do?

A gunshot broke the melee. A cloud of blue smoke settled around Purdy and the two men. Wide eyed, his heart pounding in his throat, Craft leaned forward on the steering wheel to stare in disbelief at them. Purdy was still standing, so were the other two. Purdy must have punctuated his orders with the shot, Craft decided as he slumped in relief under the steering wheel.

The two brothers, their hands raised high, marched toward the car ahead of Purdy.

"There's been a mistake," a distraught woman shrieked. "They never done it!"

Purdy looked unfazed by her pleading. He holstered his gun, handcuffed the silent prisoners and then loaded them in the back seat.

"Young man, let's see if you can get this thing back to Sulphur," he finally said, then he climbed in.

Craft nodded, revived the engine and ground the transmission into low. It chugged around in a great U-turn away from the shouting woman, toward town and the jail. Uneventfully he delivered his passengers to the courthouse at six-ten on Purdy's great gold watch.

"Thank you, young man," Purdy said after unloading his prisoners. "The sheriff will pay you your fee in the next few days."

Craft thanked him, then he proudly drove the Dodge back to the family store. Flushed with excitement, his best pals swarmed off the porch to greet him, freckle face Bobby Jack and Alvin Frank with his stubborn cowlick standing up in back like a rooster comb.

"Well, tell us all about it," Bobby Jack gushed.

"Only one shot was fired."

"One shot?" Alvin ran his hands over the fender feeling for a bullet hole.

Craft shook his head in disgust at his friend's searching. "No one shot the car silly. He fired once into the air to settle them down."

"Wow! Were you right there?"

"Close enough."

"What's he like?"

So Craft explained all Purdy had told him about cattle drives and John Wesley Hardin, as they went inside and had a sarsaparilla to celebrate his first law enforcement adventure.

ϴ ϴ ϴ

After scanning the news headlines on the front page that told how America would soon go to war against the Kaiser, Craft read the obituary, about the famous Texas ranger losing a bout with pneumonia. William Houston Purdy went to his reward in the great sky, December 18th, according to the Sulphur Valley Gazette.

The next few days, several gray-haired men gathered at the hotel to join the procession from Parnell's funeral parlor to the hill cemetery where they took the deceased. From the store front window, Craft watched the old timers shuffle long-faced up Weather Street.

He studied the saddled buckskin horse trailing behind the hearse and approved of it. Then he turned on his heel and went back to finish stocking shelves—another legend was gone like a dust devil spun away into oblivion.

Later in the afternoon, he looked up from his sweeping when Sheriff Micheals came through the front door, tingling the bell. The man's broad shoulder's crowded the brown suit. Craft realized the lawman had a purpose and he was the person he sought.

"You must have impressed the old man," the sheriff began.

"Pardon sir?"

"Bill Purdy. He left some strict instructions."

"Oh." Craft blinked in confusion as Micheals held the great gold watch before him.

"Take it. He wanted you to have it."

"Me?"

"Yes. He asked on his dying bed that the polite boy who took him on his one and only car ride should have it. You know old Billy never said much, but I guess he was sure impressed with you."

Craft acknowledged he'd heard the sheriff's words as he opened the timepiece's face with shaky fingers. Then he laid it to his ear to listen to the ticking. He'd probably never hear all those tales about Kansas, the saloon gals and famous wild places, but he did have a great watch that once belonged to an important man. Why he'd be the one in history who gave the former ranger Bill Purdy his only car ride. He polished the gleaming case on his shirtfront, then he pocketed his prized possession. Wouldn't his buddies envy him now?

A Cold Wind Cries for Her

The frost-crusted snow would not support her. Each time she stepped, her moccasin and the bare calf of her leg plunged into the icy powder beneath. Guided by the Moon of the Last Goose, Deer Woman struggled northward in the white world of night, pained by her fresh widowhood and the loss of her two children. She hastened onward in an effort of blind survival, to put as much distance as possible between her and the treacherous Yellow Legs. Under her long breasts beat the strong heart of a warrior for many times she had carried war against the Long Knives

Cold scorched her cheeks like a firebrand. Doubt fogged her mind as she breathed deep to fill her straining lungs. She needed to find a warm friendly lodge. Her own tepee was a charred ring, no doubt hidden already by the wind driven snow.

Early that day, the pony soldiers raked their village with grape shot from a cannon, then they charged in to kill the survivors. Her tall handsome husband Red Horse lay dead, a crimson wound in his chest that seeped onto his quill vest. Both of her children stilled and bloody beyond recognition from the fierce blasts of the cannon shot. Even before the madmen on horseback raced screaming into their camp, she had suffered her losses.

"Death you Indian bitch!" The trooper charged from out of nowhere, bearing down on her, but he snapped an empty pistol and the speed of his horse carried him by her. Bewildered at how to escape amid the death, raping, scalping and screams of her people, she managed somehow to step in the right places and soon found herself burrowed into a cavity between two dead Indian ponies at the edge of

camp. The sorrow burned inside her as she concealed
herself, forced to clutch her fingers so tightly the nails dug
into her palms to contain the urge to rise up and kill
everyone of the blue coats.

She tried to shut out the cries of pain. Even with her
hands over her ears she still heard the survivors pleading
under the brutal hands of the soldiers. Fervently, she asked
her spirits to deliver her people from this hell, but her gods
did not answer her. The cries went on forever.

Under the cover of darkness, she slipped away from this
place of death. The obscene talk of the white eyed soldiers
around blazing fires carried across the frozen prairie as she
stole her way up a draw to leave the scene of so much
devastation. There remained nothing she could do for Red
Horse or her small children—the knot in her throat
restricted her breathing as she bent low running away
from her losses. The bitter smoke of smoldering lodges
branded the inside of her nose; she would never forget the
sickening smell of burning buffalo hide and hair.

Cold night air knifed her lungs as she hurried westward,
determined, despite the burden of sorrow, to live. The
spirits had saved her for a purpose and although she did
know the true nature of their wishes she did not doubt that
her survival was planned by the Gods of her world. Even as
her moccasins crunched the snow, her future was not clear
to her. Deer Woman pushed into the night—away from the
treacherous white eyes.

Dawn dazzled across her frigid world. Afraid of their
pursuit, she often glanced back over her shoulders. Each
time, her heart stopped for a beat when she re-visualized
the distorted face of the pony soldier snapping his empty
pistol at her and at any moment expecting to die from his
bullet that never came. Hugging the trade blanket around
her shoulders, she hurried on.

To survive, she must ration the meager buffalo jerky in her elk skin dress pockets. The substance needed to last her many days until she found another camp of her own people. Grateful the small streams were frozen solid, she quickly crossed another, labored up the steep bank and moved on again.

At last, she stopped to recapture her breath, then squinted against the blinding glare. Something was out there on her back trail, she had seen it move. Her heart rate quickened at the notion—the relentless ones had scented and found her back trail. Only a flash and then a shadow, but she knew they would be coming for her; buffalo wolves were on her tracks. Her hand closed on the handle of the sharp knife in her belt. Even keen edged steel would be no match for the slashing teeth of the predators. Perhaps she could find a tall tree to stay in during the night, but there were none in sight and she didn't expect to find one.

She hurried on, grateful for her powerful, long legs. As a girl she could out run most boys. Tall for a Sioux woman, she stood a head higher above most of her tribesmen, except her beloved Red Horse who was the tallest male of the Mandan people. When she looked back for signs of her pursuers she felt a deep twinge of remorse over the loss of that powerful man. Never again would Red Horse part her legs and send her into the land of passion.

The things she treasured were all gone, her husband, their two children, the great tepee that turned the north wind and their horse herd. Deer Woman felt pangs of guilt for not remaining and giving her family a proper burial. The spirits would have to forgive her. Besides they had sent her in headlong flight away from the destroyed camp into the fangs of the buffalo wolves who would kill her and shred her body into bloody parts for their own pleasure.

The slinkers on her back trail grew braver as the day lengthened. Despite the cold, the sun warmed her left side through the layers of blanket and leather. She appreciated the warmth. Still the breath escaping her lips turned to vapor and the sun's glare burned her eyes.

After darkness fell on the snowfields, the cowardly yellow eyes would come in snarling and snipping at her. Finally when she could no longer scare them away with her screaming threats and the knife, they would charge in. First the leaders would shred her bare calves under the elk skin dress as they sought to pull her down. At the same time, she would be trying to fend them away from jumping at her tender throat while they tore at her back. With her finally down on the snow, the wolves would get braver, despite her screams. The copper smell of her wounds and the success of the braver ones would feed the desire of the others to rush in. Without honor, her blood would stain the snow as she died.

Their final attack, she knew, would not occur until after sunset. She raced to the next ridge and paused to catch her breath, she looked back across the sea of dazzling ice. The wolves were back there. Mere dark specs pacing back and forth in place. She even imagined seeing their great red tongues lolled out as they panted, acting bored. Waiting for her to go forth, wear herself down some more; they were patient killers and would follow.

Woman Deer with her leather skirt in her hands, plowed on with long strides. She hoped to see the smoke of another winter camp when she reached the next high point. She wished to find lodges of friends and relatives where she could share her losses before a warming fire. The leader of her camp, Chief Yellow Sleeve was dead too.

Finally on the crest, she shaded her eyes with the sides of her hands; she saw no camp—only more whiteness. She also knew viewing the empty land, when the sunset finally fell to her left, the wolves would close in and her life would end.

No one to hear her screams, She pledged in silence to die honorably. Soon she must find herself a place to make the final stand against the blood thirsty ones. Even for her own death she must plan.

The tormentors grew braver. They were finally close enough that when she stopped to gulp more air, she could see their long red tongues. However they would not look at her. Their yellow eyes averted from her stare. She knew when they sprung for her throat they would look at her. A shudder of raw fear made her shoulders quake.

The flat report of a powerful rifle forced her to whirl to see the shooter. The soldiers had found her. Deer Woman did not recognize the buckskin-clad figure as she floundered to stand in the deep snow. He stood in the stirrups to take aim and fired again at the confused wolves.

They savagely attacked the stricken member of the pack that yelped in pain from his wound and the bites of his pack mates. Some cowered close by, unsure whether to attack their brother or flee.

The stranger's powerful black horse breathed great clouds of vapor and the string of horses heavily laden with packs remained behind him. His rifle belched more smoke and death. Another wolf pitched down and died without a whimper. The wounded one still cried, but the last shot proved to be enough for the other lobos. They left in great leaps racing across the sun's glare to escape the brand of death that he dispensed.

Would he kill her next? She wondered as her hand closed on the antler handle of the knife in her belt. Filled with distrust she silently promised she would die honorably and proud. It made no difference, she would not beg for her life.

"Hey, where is your horse?" he asked, sitting down in the Mexican saddle and holstering the long gun in its boot.

She did not blink. Deer Woman understood English but if he was to kill her—why should she talk to this man?

"Where's your camp?" he asked an edge of anger creeping into his voice. "Are you speechless?" he demanded.

She teetered dizzy with exhaustion. Her strong resolve locked her knees and she vowed not to faint, nor to show this white eye any weakness. Despite her teeth clenched effort, her vision began to swarm and the snow came up fast to meet her.

"Christ, woman are you losing a baby?" he demanded as she tried to raise up. No good, she fluttered away into the sleep of the pained.

He had bound her. She tried to move her limbs and couldn't. The white eye had tied her up tight and intended to feed her to the wolves. What was she constricted in—she did feel warm and there was a fire. "Ah, you're coming around," he spoke and she began to realize they were inside a small lodge. "Here, I'll help you." he offered, but she tried to draw away.

"Suit your self, I ain't all that fond of you either," he said and relighted his pipe with a sliver of wood from the fire.

The smoke was sweet and she wondered what things he burned for it smelled settling despite her position. The blankets, she was wrapped in were his too, for the material carried the scent of a white man and that tobacco. Certainly not an Indian male either. She soon discovered the blankets weren't bonds and fell away; he had merely wrapped her tight to hold in her body heat while she slept.

"I have food."

She did not answer though her empty stomach hurt.

"You can go on being stupid or you can eat a bowl of my cooking." On his haunches, he waited ready to dip her some from the kettle swung over the fire.

"White eyes killed my man and children two days ago," she said.

"Injuns killed my woman and a papoose a month ago."

"You had an Indian wife?" she asked, touching the ground for her balance as she settled on her haunches.

"Part Injun."

"Who killed her, the Pawnees?"

"No, the Sioux."

"My people?"

"It don't make a damn—everyone is killing everyone in this damn crazy world up here." He gave her a look of disgust.

A rawboned burly man, but powerful for he had carried her to this lodge. She could see the night sky and stars out the smoke hole. How long had she been unconscious? She needed to go outside and relieve her bladder. Would he let her go? He did not appear cruel.

"I will go out and come back," she said waiting on his nod. He settled back and she left him.

The cold air shocked her when she emerged from the lodge. She waded past the close tied horses. What did her spirits want her to do? This man did not seem murderous. Still her recent losses forced her to dread any white. She did not stay outside long for the cold felt worse and the snow much deeper.

She ducked back inside and slung a blanket over her shoulders to restore some of the lost warmth. He looked at her expectantly and she bobbed her head that she would try his food. On his knees, he dipped her out a full bowl and handed it to her.

The rich smelling dish in her hands, she nodded thanks and wondered if underneath the bushy red beard there was a chin and a face. She had seen his mouth under the bow of his mustache and the even line of white teeth.

Deer Woman began to recall his panic when he first found her. He'd asked, was she losing a child? No, she carried no child. Head bowed, she waited for the steaming stew to cool. Even though he was white, she owed him her life—she paused. The spirits had sent her to him; she stared at him for a long second. No, surely they had not taken her children and husband in such a cruel way so she might serve this bushy faced man—the knowledge caused a sickness in the pit of her belly that settled like a great stone. She had read the signs careful enough and the notion bothered her more than she wanted to admit.

"Where are your people?"

"Blue legs kill all of them."

"They're closing in on all the wild ones."

She shook her head. "Not wild ones, we are on the land our gods have given us."

"White man's taking all that back."

"It's not his!"

"Don't matter, he has guns and the army and the Sioux too will bend."

"We want none of his res-va-tions."

He filled his pipe and looked at her with a hardness that struck her heart like flint and steel. "Then try the happy hunting grounds, that's where the free ones are."

"Better to be dead then," she said and set the food down.

"Eat your food," he said then he lighted the finger packed tobacco with a great sulfurous match.

"You are not my boss!"

"You are my woman now," he said, before letting a small stream of the sweet smoke hiss from his teeth.

"I am no man's woman!"

He pointed the stem at her. "You have no choice, it's either me or the wolves and I have a warmer lodge."

"What will you do with me?" she demanded.

He frowned in displeasure. "Sell you to a Crow if you don't settle down."

"No never! I would not ever be a slave in their camp."

"You talk like a woman that's got a helluva lot of options."

"Op-tions?" She did not know such a word.

"Meaning you can either go out there and feed them hungry wolves or keep this lodge with me."

"My man has—"

"Don't matter, you and I are alive and that's what counts. What's your name?"

"Deer Woman."

"Red Lyon."

"You are part big cat?" She looked at him hard.

"No, just Red Lyon, my name is not an animal."

Deer nodded she understood and picked up the bowl. He was a dominant man and she knew she did not dare to trifle with him. The stew drew her saliva as she considered her fate. He had food and a warm place, she should be grateful for him finding her despite the burden of her sorrows.

Deer Woman did not share the Lyon's blankets though she assumed the role of his helper. He moved them southward for several days journey. Astride a powerful horse, she led the pack string. She hoped to see some of her own kind but after many familiar miles with the Big Horn Mountains to the sunset side of her body—she saw no camps of the Sioux. Not finding any sign of her people drove her sorrow deeper—maybe the army had killed all of them. At every turn in the way, she was reminded of the lifeless bodies of her family. She bowed her head and beat her heels on the big horse's ribs for him to go faster.

They met three breeds in late afternoon. The threesome stared at her with hungry intentions as they sat their skinny horses breathing clouds of vapors in the cold.

"We'll take her for some of our robes," the thin-faced one laughed. The cruel glint in his eyes undressed her and made Deer shudder under the thick warm blanket that she wore for a coat.

"Not for sale," Lyon said.

"Ten robes!" the breed shouted, acting angry that Lyon did not take him serious.

"She is not for sale." Lyon shifted his coat and she knew the great ivory-handed pistol in his belt was exposed for him to draw and fire.

"You are crazy! She's a damn Sioux! She'll split your throat some night in your sleep. I know how to treat them." Then the man shared another smirk with the other two who looked warmed to the notion of having her for their own purposes.

"I will trade for your pelts," Lyon shook his head, "but not the woman."

"You have powder and lead?" the Breed asked but he could hardly keep from snatching looks at her.

Lyon agreed and they spent the afternoon bartering on a blanket, despite the falling temperature, they acted like they were very deliberate in their trading. Deer knew that they only stalled for darkness to come—did Lyon know this?

The hairy-faced man had suddenly become her responsibility—yes, he was the key to saving her from the three schemers who by her estimation were hardly better than the wolves. She must help Lyon watch, for they would murder him in a minute for his horses, and goods, including her. Their presence made her skin tingle as she poured them coffee. She side stepped as one reached to put his hand on her thigh.

"We have some white otter," the leader said with a grin.

Lyon nodded he had heard. "How many?"

"Three and they are prime."

"Very rare," Lyon said as the youngest one brought them.

"Five gold pieces," the Breed said. He waited ready to pounce on Lyon's offer in return.

"Too high!"

"Then I give them for the woman!" he shouted and held the snowy pelts high over his head.

"She's not for sale!"

"You have had her. We have been away from a woman's flanks for many moons. Give her to us for one night." The others agreed with quick nods as they waited for his answer.

"How many times must I say no!"

"We are through trading with you!" the head one said in disgust and rose to his feet.

"Those white furs?"

"Never!" he snarled and they stomped to his horses. In a bound, they mounted and gave Lyon a cross look. Deer nearly laughed at them as she drew the oily smelling buffalo gun from the saddle boot and brought it to him.

"Thanks Deer," he said with his hard stare locked on the threesome as they lashed their animals away in a flurry of snow and left them.

"They will be back," she said and bent over the fire to stoke it.

"They will only come back to die," he said and she looked up at the resolve in his green eyes. He would kill them without a blink of his eyelids.

"The white skins," she said, "are worth three squaws?"

He agreed with a small nod, still watching them. She looked as they went over the high rise, their horses fighting the deep snow.

Night came early as it did in the Last Moon of the Goose. A wolf howled to his pack on the mountain. The hair rose on her scalp as she sat in the lodge and brushed her hair by firelight. He came inside and set the rifle down.

"No snow tonight, it's clear out there. They'll come back during the night."

"What will we do?"

"Go outside, lay down by the packs and kill them when they come for us."

"You could have sold me?" she asked.

"Why?" he asked. "Those breeds would have hurt you."

She shrugged her shoulders and stared in the fire. "Anyone can be a worker. Even a boy could do what work I do for you."

He roughly raised her by the arm and looked deep in her eyes. "When you stop mourning for your family, then you tell me, until then, be quiet."

She blinked her eyes at his words. Without saying anything else, he began gathering blankets to go outside. She wondered what he meant—forget her family. She would always be sad for the loss, though the pain was less. Should she still be in mourning? A guilty lance struck her conscience. Red Horse, the children, they seemed further away although she missed them; she wanted a man's strong arms to hold her as the memory of her husband's affection grew dimmer.

"Get the canvas sheets, that will be our cover. First, build up the fire so they'll think we're in here."

Deer nodded she understood as she fueled the campfire. Lyon was setting a trap. They had not fooled him either. She ducked low to go outside with her arms loaded down. The cold air slapped her into seriousness. The night was frigid as any that season.

In their hiding place among the panniers they waited belly down, side by side in a wedge of blankets. The sharp wind drove hard grains of ice at them as they lay poised, ready for the attackers. The frozen flecks made ticking sounds striking on the material over them. She wished for the comfort of the lodge which shed much of winter's force. but she knew the canvas cover would pass for snow if the breeds did not examine it too closely.

The night passed slowly and the moon was nearly set when she heard voices on the wind.

"They come," she said then buried her tingling face in the buffalo robe beneath them for a moment to warm it.

He handed her the pistol. "Can you shoot it?"

She nodded.

"Be sure who you shoot," he said and rolled over on his side to cock the rifle.

The breeds' shots made her start. She saw the orange blazes from their rifles as they came down the hillside shooting at the conical lodge. His hand quickly stayed her. Two of them were edging closer, shadowy figures on the albino slope. She carefully cocked the hammer back waiting his order.

Her stomach crawled as she tried to squint to better see their silhouettes. They had stopped to reload. Metal cartridges clicking loudly as they injected them and they talked triumphantly about there being no sign of life in the lodge.

They were less than thirty feet when he gave the command, "Now!" and raised up.

She pointed the barrel and thumbed the hammer back for each shot as the pair withered to the snow in a hail of their gunfire. Then there was silence except the quiet clicks as her man reloaded the pistol for her.

"You did good," he mumbled and handed her back the Colt.

"The other one is not here?" she asked.

"I have to go find him," Lyon said, impatiently searching about the silver world that held them.

Deer reached out and grasped his arm to make him stay for a moment. "After this you plan to go to places like Fort Laramie?"

"Why?" he asked acting anxious to go find the last breed, who probably held their horses beyond the last hill.

"White men leave their Indian woman at such places."

"So?"

"You promise to kill me when you grow tired of me?"

He looked into her eyes. "You're saying I must kill you if I ever get tired of you?"

Deer nodded aggressively. "I don't want to die drinking bad whiskey and lying with soldiers."

"I understand," he said. "Now I must go find the other one."

She agreed. "You come back. There will be one bed in your lodge."

"Yes, I won't be long then." He started out across the gray snow, then stopped and turned back. His words soft spoken over the night wind. "Deer Woman, I won't ever leave you or kill you either one."

Deer heard his promise as she shook the dry snow from her blankets. She must arrange the lodge special for his return. From here on, she must care for this man—half Sioux children would be better than no Sioux. Her ear turned to better hear the night sounds, she listened to the whispers of the wind and hoped her spirits someday would tell her why they had delivered her to him. She felt certain it was their wishes that she be with this man as she went inside her lodge to wait for his return.

Room For Two

The wind bore needles of ice that struck his canvas coat like spears. Even with his sheepskin collar turned up, the chill still invaded the security of his wool shirt and mixed with his perspiration, causing him to shiver. He was grateful the funeral service was over. His nearest neighbor Herman Peterson had suffered enough; death was a blessing in this man's case.

Thurman Lake looked with pity at the bent figure in the old blue army overcoat with her head wrapped in a black scarf, it was hard to tell she was a woman. Though past twenty, Dunkia Peterson had never married. First, her mother, then her father had lingering illnesses; the young girl had grown into a woman while caring for their needs.

Thurman recalled seeing her the past spring in a wash worn dress and men's pants beneath it, following a mismatched team with a steel hand plow. She made a rawboned figure, shoulders too wide, and her straw colored short hair tossed by the spring wind. Cheeks raw from the elements, she hadn't looked up when he rode up that spring day. He only stopped to ask her how the old man was doing.

"Papa has good days," she said. Her downcast gaze centered on the soil scoured shinny plowshare.

"Planting oats?" he asked.

She nodded woodenly.

He had said something else to her then, but he could not remember what. Thurman could not find any words to comfort her this day as much as he regretted his inadequacy. Leaning into the wind, he fought his way to the huddled wooly-coated mustang. He made two tries to mount his horse, but his boot soles were so icy, they slipped from the stirrup. When at last mounted, he lifted the reins and headed the gelding home. To conserve his body heat, Thurman bent over in the saddle.

His spread was two hours away, three in the snow and cold. By the time he arrived, the weak dying sun shone across the flat grey snow.

In the protected alleyway of the cottonwood log barn, he dismounted. His back muscles were contracted stiff from his fight with the cold. For more circulation, Thurman stomped his numb feet on the bare frozen ground before he unsaddled his horse. After he put the Texas saddle on the rack in the feed room, he tossed the horse three ears of corn as a reward.

The path to the small house had drifted over with four inches of dry snow. When he swung the corral gate shut to contain his horse, the leather hinges protested louder than the wind.

In his absence the fire had gone down. His breath produced streams of vapor as he poked the few remaining coals in the stove. With a small scoop, he added coal from the packing crate bin. Then he pulled off his heavy mittens, and slipped off the plaid wool cap. It would soon be warm inside. He undid the deer antler buttons of his coat. Darkness began to engulf the room before he lighted the kerosene lamp

He busied himself with meal preparation. First, he sliced bacon from the slab. While it fried, he went after potatoes from the house's cellar. After supper, he blew out the lamp. Wearily in the darkness he pulled off his boots, shed his waist overalls, and then climbed between the quilts and the feather mattress. His last thoughts before he fell asleep were that in the morning he must feed his cows.

Before the sun cracked the North Dakota morning, he rose from the warm covers, charged the stove, and left a yellow stain in the snow a few feet from his door. He hated to empty the chamber pot, so he usually braved the elements.

After his oatmeal, he sipped coffee from a stained mug and waited for the sun to come up.

When he left the house, Thurman knew the temperature was well below zero. He hoped the draft horses hadn't strayed too far. Sometimes, on the mornings he fed, they came in for a reward of corn. Otherwise, he saddled the mustang and went in search of them. He repeated this ritual every third winter day.

An hour later, the big pale red Percherons were harnessed, their nostrils blowing streams of fog as they stomped their pie plate sized hooves. Trace chains jingled and leather creaked when Thurman turned them with the lines in one hand and the heavy double trees in the other. Outside, beside the barn, he sawed them back and pinned in the double tree. He was always cautious least the team bolt and jerk the big hay sled on top of him. The first few hours that he drove the Percherons, they were always too anxious.

He stood up on the boards of the sleigh and clicked to them. The team churned puffs of powdery snow with their high steps. A smile of pride touched the corners of his mouth; he enjoyed the power of his big horses.

At the wire gate to the meadows, he tied the reins to the headboard and marched ahead to open it. Beyond, the distant bare cottonwoods stood like sticks along the frozen creek. In the bottoms, the white-mantled haystacks rose in mounds.

Loading the sweet smelling fodder on the sled was hard work, but Thurman thrived on the labor. Warmed by the exertion, he tossed pitchforks of the summer's growth on to the sled. Fine grains of ice shook loose and melted on his face as he heaved the bundles higher on the load.

At last, when no more would stay on, he stuck the fork in the front so he didn't lose it. Then he untied the lines and let the team test the load. On the first try, the horses fell back as if shocked that they could not move the sleigh.

He spoke sharply to them. When they lowered themselves and their powerful ham muscles strained, the runners began to ease forward. Though Thurman knew they could do it, he still took pride at their effort. He walked beside the load and drove them south to where his herd sought shelter in the small hills.

At the gate, he let the horses blow. They were still two miles from the pole feeders that he knew would have been eaten down, but never empty. A storm might cause him not to be able to feed for several days, so he left more fodder than his hundred head could consume in three short winter days.

Past noon, the hayracks were over flowing; the she stock crowded the fresh hay as if it was sweeter than ordinary. His bulls stood back as if they considered themselves snobs and better than the foolish females. Observing their roan coats as thick as their Scottish Shorthorn ancestors, Thurman knew his sires were still well conditioned, despite the winter's onslaught.

One male arched his full neck to show his muscles as if the others or anyone cared. Then he bawled in a deep husky voice to challenge the icy hills around them. Thurman clucked to the Percherons and they swept the empty sled north and homeward. Their hard work done, anxious for the waiting meal of corn, the team churned up the white powder.

The temperature had climbed by his estimate to a little above zero. Even the wind lost its edge as he closed the last gate and clucked to the horses to go home. So far this winter, the wolves had not pulled down a single cow. He had reason to celebrate. The afternoon's low sun felt warm on the right side of his face. Maybe he'd have a glass or two of rye when he was through for the day.

At the barn, he unhitched and removed the harness. Then he picked a half bushel of corn in the shuck from the bin. He tossed a few ears out in the alleyway for the mustang to eat before he took the big horses outside the corral.

Beyond the gate he poured the corn on the ground for them, took off their work bridles and went back to put them in the tack room. The mustang was already eating his share, his molars noisily crushing the flinty kernels as Thurman went around him. His day's work complete, he dropped the tack room latch in place and headed for his house.

There was still an hour's light left. Thurman considered what he would cook for supper. In the morning he planned to ride north and hunt for a mule deer. A month's supply of venison would make the trip worthwhile.

Thurman stomped his boots as he opened the door. In dismay, he blinked his glare burned eyes. Seated at the table in the cold room was Dunkia. She did not raise her scarf bound head at his entry.

"Why didn't you put coal in the stove?" he asked, angry at her backwardness. Thurman opened the cast iron door and shoveled in the dark chunks with a ferocity to match his mood. Anyone should know they were welcome to fuel his stove. To just sit there and be cold—what was the matter with her?

"It wasn't my coal," she quietly mumbled.

"Next time," he said sharply. "Use some of mine". Free of his mittens and cap, he undid the buttons on his coat. She must be simple, he decided. Thurman dared not look at her. He wondered how she had found his place: she'd never been there before.

"I had no place to go," she said.

He studied her. With the wool scarf wrapped around her bowed head, she huddled in the old blue army coat. To him, she looked small and defenseless.

"Don't you have your farm?" he asked, shrugging off his coat.

"No. The bank has taken it."

Thurman frowned and shook his head. "Bastards!" he swore under his breath. What sort of low life turned a girl out in the cold?

"I owed them more money than I could ever pay. They let me stay until papa died. It was an understanding."

Her explanation hardly settled the issue for him. She must have known for a long while that after the old man's death they would evict her.

"You can stay here," he said, even before he thought. What had he offered? One room, one bed, one chamber pot, one everything—this was no place for two.

"I could go to work in town," she said. Her voice sounded full of dread.

Thurman looked at her. Dunkia clearly meant Sophie's place. He could not imagine her in a filmy gown seated in the parlor, coaxing men to hardness and leading them back to a cubicle. No, he did not think she could do that.

"You can stay here," he said. He would not have her loss of respectability on his conscience. Dunkia might be backward, but she didn't fit his image of a soiled dove.

He hung his coat and cap on a peg by the door. Maybe she thought he wanted her for that reason.

"I can cook." He heard her say before he turned around.

"Good," he said, feeling grateful that she had broken the silence.

The room was warming, but she did not offer to remove her scarf or coat. He scowled at her.

"Take off your coat," he said, sharper than he intended.

The chair legs scrapped the floor as she rose unsteady to obey him. Her frost burned red fingers fumbled with the odd buttons. She slipped out of the coat, and he took it, waiting for her to undo the scarf.

He remembered the wash worn dress from the day he spoke to her in the oat field. She looked thinner; her bones seemed to hold up the wash worn material. He turned and went to put her outer clothes on the peg beside his own.

"What should I cook?" she asked.

"There are potatoes in the cellar." He pointed to the trap door in the floor. "I'll cut some bacon."

"How many?" she asked.

"Four or five," he finally said. "There are plenty. And get a jar of plums."

"Yes."

He sliced the white fat in layers off the brown slab and into the skillet on the stove. She came up from below with her hand full of the red spuds.

"You have so much food," she said.

"Plenty," he said. In truth, though Thurman never thought about his store beneath the house, there was easily enough for two. Obviously, Dunkia was impressed.

"Do you like bread?" she asked. "Tomorrow, I can bake some for you."

"Sure," he said. He watched her wash each individual potato with her thumb erasing the last trace of dirt. Her hands were so raw and cracked that he hurt for her. He stepped back when she indicated for him to move aside so she could slice the potatoes over the hot grease.

She was deft with his sharp knife, the white slices swiftly dropping into the sizzling skillet. When she finished, she said, "I'll go get the plums."

"Yeh." Thurman wished the house were larger so they could keep a distance. Perhaps with more space she would be more at ease.

Thurman noticed the sun was about to set. Red rays danced on the frost patterns etched on the front window. He lighted the lamp. As he replaced the glass chimney, the strong coal oil smell filled his nose. A bit of smoke blackened the narrow throat, so he adjusted the flat wick until he was satisfied. He mused how different it would be with her in his house.

He took a dog eared journal from the stack and sat at the table, pretending to read it. He knew every page by heart but he pretended to concentrate so she would not feel so self-conscious.

"Do you want coffee?' she asked.

"Sure." He wondered why he had not thought of it. If he had been alone, he would already be drinking some. His molars floated at the notion of hot coffee in his dry mouth. He closed the journal and returned it to the pile. With his hands shoved flat in his front pants pockets, he teetered on his boot heels at a loss for how he should act towards her.

She set the table, but never looked up at him as if she were too busy. But he, in turn, felt all the more obvious about standing idly by.

"It is done," she announced. She placed the skillet on the table, using a rag to protect her hand.

He sat down and dug in; fishing out some bacon and spearing a few brown potatoes. Thurman stopped when he realized that she was still standing.

"Sit down and eat," he said.

The chair bumped as she took her place opposite him. After she sat, he finished filling his plate.

"I can go to town," she said.

"We settled that. You are staying here." He did not look at her as he began to eat.

When he heard her sniff, he glanced up. Her lashes were wet.

"Eat," he said pointing at her plate with his fork.

"If I can," she mumbled.

Thurman frowned at her words. He leaned back and considered her.

"Were you starving?" he asked.

Her nod was enough to sicken him. She was not only homeless, but hungry. He was shocked by the truth of her situation. They'd had no food. The picture dulled his appetite. If she hadn't come, she might have died and he would never have known of her plight. This new knowledge depressed him.

"Coffee?" she asked with the graniteware poised over his mug.

Thurman nodded. He watched the brown liquid splash in the cup. Even the rich tasting coffee did not seem much of a treat for him at the moment.

As he lifted his mug to blow the steam away, he studied her bobbed straw colored hair. She must have brushed it a hundred times for it shown in the lamplight. He realized how she must have feared he would reject her while she had waited all day for him to return.

When their meal was finished, she busied herself gathering the dishes. Deliberate, Dunkia paused when she reached for his plate.

"I forgot the plums," she said.

"They'll be good for breakfast," he said.

"You do not have to be kind to me," she said.

Thurman blinked at her. "Huh?"

"I will do your bidding under your roof. If I do things wrong or forget, I expect you to punish me."

"We'll see," he said. Feeling his face heat up, he was relieved that she had taken his plate and turned her back. He noticed she was washing the dishes in steaming water from the stove. Then he remembered the can of petroleum jelly that might soothe her raw hands.

On his knees, Thurman dug through the chest. Finally he found the small tin, with its label nearly worn off down to the metal. He pushed himself up to his feet

"Here..." he said, realizing she was pouring more water in the dishpan atop the dry sink.

"The dishes are done," she said softly. "If you will turn your head, I'll clean up."

"Sure," he said as he turned. Her words made him feel as if he had violated her privacy.

"I won't be long," she assured him.

Take all the time you want, he mused to himself. His attention centered on the frost patterns that etched the window glass. After a few minutes, he heard her say that she was finished and Thurman remembered the greasy can in his hand.

"This may help your hands," he said and crossed the room to hand it to her.

"Mister Lake?" she said.

"Yes?"

"You are being very kind to me."

He shrugged her gratitude away. She snapped off the lid and took a small dab on the end of her fingertip. Impatient with her timidness, Thurman stepped closer, took the can and dipped three of his fingers in the ointment. Then he took her hand and rubbed the grease in the back of it. Lord, he shuddered, she'd be all day doing any good.

"As dry as your hands are," he said. "A little isn't going to do it."

Busy working it in, he barely heard her soft, "Yes."

Then realizing he was touching her for the first time, he became self-conscious. But determined to ease her condition, he kept massaging the jell in.

When he finished, they were standing very close. Her slick hands were still in his light grasp as he looked into her sky blue eyes. He leaned closer to her face, expecting her to twist her head. But to his surprise, Dunkia held her place for him to kiss her on the lips. The moment was brief and when he opened his eyes, he felt shaken by his own forwardness.

If he ever wanted to make a sincere sounding statement, the time seemed at hand. The moment passed and he stepped back instead, releasing her hands. Words never came. Instead he blew out the lamp and plunged the room into darkness.

"You take this side of the bed," he announced. "I'll take the other side."

As he sat down in the chair to take off his boots, she moved past him. In the silver starlight, he could barely see Dunkia unbuttoning her dress.

What in hell's name would she sleep in? It just wasn't any worry of his. He strained to pull off his left boot. When he looked up again, her silhouette was gone, but the protest of the bed told him enough. His second one came off even harder. Maybe this sleeping in the same bed wasn't such a good idea?

He'd expected her to sleep fully dressed. Surely, he told himself, she has under clothes on. When he stood up, he considered shedding his britches, but decided against it and went around to his side.

Thurman drew a deep breath, then raised the quilts and edged in. When his hip touched hers, he moved an inch away, pulled up the covers, and settled on his left side. Good enough, he decided.

"Mister Lake?" she asked softly.

"Yes?"

"Do you always sleep in your clothes?"

Thurman sat straight up and slapped the covers with his palms. "Quit calling me mister! My name's Thurman and I usually sleep in my long johns."

"Yes, Thurman."

"And quit..." He wasn't sure what he wanted to tell her next. In disgust, he rose and took off his shirt and pants in haste.

"Now I'm like I usually sleep," he announced and climbed back in the bed with his back to her. When he was close to falling asleep, his hand dropped off his side and brushed her silky bare skin. He drew it back as if he had burned himself.

Damn, he swore silently. She was naked as a baby. He squeezed his eyelids shut. Then he scolded himself for having acted like a foolish schoolboy and kissing her. He considered getting up.

"Dunkia?" he asked softly, hoping that she was asleep and wouldn't answer him.

"Yes, Thurman." She sounded wide-awake to him.

He laid firmly on his left side without any intention of turning over until all this was settled.

"There isn't a preacher in town and I can't leave this place for more than two days because of feeding my cows. So going to the county seat is out until spring. Do you understand?"

"No."

What did he have to do, draw her a picture?

"What I'm getting at—well if you want, I'll marry you then."

"You don't have to do that mister... Thurman," she corrected herself.

He bolted to a sitting position again and stared across the dark room. "Well, I will if you'll let me!"

"Let you what?"

"Marry you, silly. Hell, I ain't even sure of what I mean."

"I will marry you," she said and pulled on his arm for him to be with her.

He half fell on top of her and braced himself so he did not crush her. A cold shiver ran up Thurman's spine. When he lowered his face to find her lips, he couldn't recall ever kissing anyone sweeter in all of his thirty-seven years.

The Last Ride

"One of old man Shurer's horses foundered, so he can't pull the hearse," Ratch said and booted his cowpony up closer to the picket gate. "They'd sure appreciate it if you'd hitch up a team and haul old Shorty's remains out to the cemetery this afternoon."

"Man, Ratch," Jeff said, his mind full of doubts about the task. "All I've got around here is an unbroken team of gray broncs. Sold my good team last week."

Ratch was not to be deterred. "Why I'll come by and we can snub them to old Brad. He's powerful enough and they can't run off with him and a wagon."

Shorty's widow Cora had been through enough. Old Shorty went off to Crosses to trade some horses. Word came back Shorty had died in his sleep. Must have been a heart attack, Jeff decided. Anyway the family needed him planted and the funeral was that afternoon. He better help them.

He told Ratch he would harness the grays while he went after his big bay and be ready in thirty minutes. His friend agreed to go by and tell the undertaker they could handle it, then return to help him manage the Unbroken pair. On his stiff right leg, Jeff hobbled around the house to the pens out back. The whole matter of using the untrained ponies niggled him, but he tried to shrug away his gut wrenching concerns.

In the corral, he lassoed the one called Goose, and she flew backwards. Her butt crashed into the pole corral and set her down on her haunches. Then she put on a head slinging fit until he managed to fashion a halter over her ears and lead her out. With her tied at the rack, still eaten

69

up with anxiety, he went back for the second one. Tyrone proved no easier and after another struggle, at last, the gelding stood snubbed to the hitching rack beside Goose. Jeff knew he'd used up the thirty minutes he'd promised and still did not have the broncs harnessed.

Ratch soon returned and eared them down while he slung on the harness and strapped it on them. The two were finally hitched to the weather beaten farm wagon; both men paused to catch their breaths and to consider their effort. Sweat ran down Jeff's face and he wiped it off on his sleeve. He wanted to ask Ratch to forget the whole thing, for the dancing gray ponies looked mighty like a hornet's nest of trouble to him. Too late for that, He climbed on the seat while his partner snubbed them up to his big stout horse.

"Ready?" Ratch asked, looking back over his shoulder.

On the seat, the lines in his hand, Jeff nodded and clucked to the team. They sashayed a little left and then right, but Ratch had them snubbed to his big bay horse which confined them to minor tricks. Down Main Street they went, dancing on their toes and acting ready to do a jig and a reel the entire two blocks to the funeral home.

When they arrived at the front door of Shurers, Jeff dared to breathe a little easier. The brake locked, lines tied off and the team snubbed close to the hitch rack, he jumped down. Still wary of them, he looked at the gray's shoulders already wet with sweat. A good day's work would kill them two. They needed several such days, he decided going inside after Ratch.

In due time, the coffin was loaded and old man Shurer talked their ears off about how much he appreciated them doing this for him and of course, for poor Mrs. Holt. Jeff agreed, anxious to have the whole thing over with, when he climbed onto the seat and undid the lines.

A few blocks away, a ball bearing mousetrap with one good eye, both ears eaten off in fights, called His Majesty, finished his dinner of a short tailed rat. His belly full and feeling nutritionally satisfied, his spring steel mind turned to thoughts of reproduction. So the gray striped male set out from the security of the area underneath the feed store floor and went west across the alley beside the adobe wall. Then using his whiskers to keep him safe from the spiny pads, he used the prickly pear fence to advance upon Montoya Street.

This wide stretch of open ground with the dirt ruts held the greatest risk for him. A mean yellow cur called Alphonso guarded the entire block against any feline invasions. The blazing sun high, His Majesty began a nimble trot over the dusty tracks. Half way across the street and feeling secure, his mind was fixed on having some amorous adventure with a gray female who was sorely needing his attention.

Then the worse sound he could ever imagine shattered the neighborhood quiet. A yellow rocket tore out of nowhere at him. His Majesty sped through Raphael Torres' yard, over a noisy pile of tin cans, leaped on his treasured tea rose bush, went over the head-high adobe wall into Sancho Blanco's yard. He raced under the brush arbor, passing beneath Sancho's wife sleeping in a hammock and around the many flats of sliced tomatoes drying in the sun.

Alphanso, not to be outdone by the cat's tactics, charged into the Blanco's yard. His sudden loud approach caused the rather plump lady to be unceremoniously dumped from the hammock to the ground. She looked up in time to see the moment the yellow invader collided with her stands. Dried tomatoes and racks flew everywhere. She scrambled to her feet with the intention of killing him. Armed with a broom, she reached the street seconds after the pair.

His Majesty decided on another diversion, though the smell proved offensive. He scrambled over the mesquite-ironwood railings and leaped in to land on top of a hundred pound shoat. Max Ickel's prize pig. The barrow's back was matted with baked on mud and at the new rider's arrival, the hog turned into a bucking horse. His squeals awoke the rest of the herd and threw them into a panic. A skinny sow breached a hole in the west wall, the rest of the herd followed. His Majesty's claws were dug in. Considering Alphonso's rapid approach, he decided to stay on his porker steed despite the bad smell and the ear shattering screams.

Down the street, ran the frightened pigs that could have outrun a racehorse. An angry yellow cur with a fat Mexican woman on his heels bound on revenge after them all. A spotted dog joined the chase. Soon others added their barking and eagerness to join in on the fun. Riding the lead hog, His Majesty looked back and wished his mount would run faster for foaming mouthed Alphonso looked to be closing in on them.

Meanwhile back at the funeral parlor, Jeff nodded to Shurer and they drove off. He felt better with the wagon underway. Ratch snubbed the dancing horses up close. They made good controlled progress for the first block.

At the second cross street Alveron, Jeff only had a moment to look up and see the wild melee coming down it. He would have sworn he saw a big gray cat riding the lead hog. Already committed to that intersection, coming out of the east were four frightened hogs, a pig riding cat, twenty barking dogs and one very out of breath Mexican woman with a broom.

It was more than the big horse Brad could stand. Ratch was forced to toss aside the lead rope. The big bay bogged his head and went off bucking down Alveron ahead of the whole pack, cat, hogs, dogs and the senora.

The grays leaped over the pigs, real and imagined. They set out in a wild run with Jeff's boot heels jammed on the footboard and him muttering short prayers. When they flew across the little used irrigation ditch, he looked back in time to see the coffin lift up and fly out the back of the wagon. Somehow, he managed to turn them in time to avoid smashing into Juan Margues' adobe hovel. In another block, he sawed them down to a trot and Ratch caught up to help him.

"You see that cat riding that hog?" Ratch asked.

Jeff shook his head. Out of strength and disgusted with his crazy unbroken horses, he had no intention of admitting he'd seen such an unbelievable sight.

"We lost Shorty," he managed.

Ratch agreed with a wary look back, then he helped him circle the team and wagon around.

From a half a block away, Jeff could see the splintered coffin. Right there in Frisco Street lay the stiff body of Shorty among the splintered boards which at one time had been his casket.

"Oh, Lord," Ratch whined as he dismounted. "What will we do now?"

Jeff set the brakes and tied off the reins. He stalked to the front to join him. His mind full of self-criticism for even offering to do this job. Stopped dead in his track, he blinked in disbelief. Whoever the corpse was, it sure wasn't Shorty Holt. He knew him.

"Ain't him," Ratch said.

"Nope."

"What will we do? His widow and the family are all waiting at the cemetery."

"Wrap whoever this is in a wagon sheet, tie it tight and let them bury the poor soul."

"But it ain't him. What do you figure happened?"

"I don't know. He died down at Hot Springs and no one knew him down there so it was probably a mix-up of the bodies."

"An honest one?" Ratch asked.

"On our part, yes."

"We better hurry or they'll think we've stolen him."

They buried "Shorty Holt" without a hitch and later placed a stone over his head. Six months later, Cora Holt married Sam Kane. They hard scrabble farmed on Shorty's old place.

Three years passed and Jeff had forgotten about the mixed up identity fracas. He and Ratch drove a cavy of horse over to southeastern Arizona. Between the Apache raids and rustlers, the price of broke horses around Tombstone was double that in West Texas. A livery man bought half of them, and two ranchers split the rest. So with their pockets full of money, they wandered down Tough Nut Street to join the Sunday crowd gathering for the cock fights.

Being strangers, they held back from the ring setup. Several handlers held their multicolored birds to await their turn in the ring. Betters frequented through the crowd waving money.

Jeff turned at the sound of a familiar voice shouting, "You Boys—"

His hand shot out and he restrained the shocked looking Ratch in time. No one in the world ever said those words exactly like that, except Shorty Holt. Turning his friend around, he pressed his fingers to his lips to quiet his partner.

"But it's him!" Ratch protested in a stage whisper.

Jeff shook his head. They must be mistaken. The red-faced man with the good-looking young Mexican girl on his arm was a dead ringer for the deceased. But Shorty was dead. They knew it, because they had hauled him to his funeral.

"That his daughter?" Ratch gasped.

"I don't think so. Maybe his niece?"

"Where're you going now?"

"Back to the saloon and have me a big drink of whiskey. I sure don't want this afternoon to turn out like the last time we had any dealings with Shorty. I don't want to see another cat come riding a runway hog down some side street leading a parade of dogs and one fat Mexican woman."

Ratch fell in beside him and laughed. "I don't either. Let's get that drink."

Rose and the Kid

Rose hitched up her low cut dress before she pushed through the batwing doors of the Silver Moon Saloon. She took a wry look around the bar room at the passed out drunken cowboys and miners. Struck with disappointment, she shook her head. Every customer in the place was either snoring open mouthed or out cold. Duffy, the barkeep stood on a chair as he lowered the wagon wheel lamp to snuff out the candles.

"It's getting late," the Irishman said. "Sorry, Rose, but there sure ain't any business for you in here."

"I can see that," she said. "Have a good night, Duffy."

"I'll have them packed out back in the alley in a little while," he said. "If you're looking for some company?"

She saw the expectancy in his eyes and smiled to console him. "Not tonight, Duff." He had expected a free toss in her bed. Perhaps another time. She turned on her heel. This had been a slow night for her. She'd managed to win a little money in a card game up the street at the Los Amigos Bar. But, she had hoped to find a cash customer at closing time. Outside the shuttered swinging doors, she paused on the porch to place her hands on her hips and stretch the tight muscles in her tired back. She dreaded the hike back to her shack on Cabbage Hill. Damn the luck. Typical middle of the month night, everyone was broke. In the cool mountain night air, she strode the dark, hollow-sounding boardwalk.

"Evening, Rose," the town marshal, Reagan said, stepping out from the shadows of a doorway.

"Hello, Reagan," she said and shot a grim glance back down the boardwalk.

"What's wrong?" Reagan asked, moving in to stand close to her. "I can tell by your voice that you're upset."

"Just one of those nights, I guess."

"What can I do for you?"

She felt the lawman's hand brush her hip and then familiar-like cup the left side of her butt. Reagan liked her, she just wasn't that certain how she felt about him. Her fingers caught his overly familiar hand in a firm grasp. Carefully, she removed it. "I owe you, don't I?" she asked.

"I'll be by in the morning to collect," he said, with a boyish grin.

Rose could read his devilish look. His words were no idle threat. In the morning, she promised herself, she would be able to tolerate him. Besides, in her business, giving free services to the law was expected. Call it payoff, whatever, she understood her place. The tradeoff was simply part of a dove's life and a necessity for survival in a frontier town. Having one of the town lawmen sweet on her was another advantage.

As she stood on the boardwalk with him, she wondered if she would ever do anything about his offer for her to move in with him? Perhaps someday.

"See you in the morning," she said and left him.

The street up Cabbage Hill was rutted from the mine wagon traffic. In the starlight, she lifted her dress hem as she climbed the steep grade past the row of darkened frame shacks.

She shouldered open the front door to her one room place. Then crossing the dark interior to the table, she felt for the familiar coal oil lamp.

"Don't light it, Rose," a man's husky voice said.

"Who's here?" she hissed. Her eyes were not adjusted to the interior darkness. Anger rose in her chest at the notion of an uninvited intruder in her cabin.

"Billy."

Billy Bonney. Her heart began to race at the realization that Billy the Kid was back. She recognized his silhouette as he stood by the window. There was no doubt, it was him.

"What are you doing back in San Marcos, so soon?" she asked, almost weak with shock.

"Is that all you can ask?" he demanded. "I came a long ways to see you."

"I'm sorry," she said, regretting her harsh words. Billy was her favorite man, even if he was a wanted, convicted killer. She considered him to be her loveable Billy. Despite the danger of his being there, she smiled, damn Bill and all his problems, he was someone special to her.

He crossed the room and took her in his arms then kissed her. For a long moment, locked in a tight hug, she forgot what problems his visit might cause and savored his mouth on hers. Same old Billy, she mused.

"That damn Pat Garrett's on my trail," he said releasing her and walking back to the window. "He keeps hounding me like a rabbit."

"Did he follow you here?" she asked.

"No. He thinks I'm in Old Mexico."

"When did you eat last? Never mind, I'll fix you some cold beans," she said, knowing that Billy never ate regular meals.

"I just needed to talk with you a little . . .I think about you a lot, Rose."

"That's nice," she said. In the trail of starlight from the window, she spooned the frijoles onto a plate for him. Billy wasn't any different than most men, Rose mused, they lied when they wanted something, like for her to crawl in bed with them. He'd probably slept with fourteen different Mexican *putas* in the past two weeks.

"You don't believe me, do you?" he asked, sitting down at the table.

"Oh, Billy," she sighed. "I'm glad you're here."

"Well, I'll just get a few hours sleep here and ride on."

"Don't act like a mistreated school boy," she said. "You can stay that long, but the town marshal's coming in the morning to visit me."

"Who's he?"

"It doesn't matter. He does favors for me," she said, not wanting to discuss the matter.

"I'll be gone by then," he said as he wolfed down his food. "Do I know him?"

"No."

"Do you see him often?" he asked in a soft voice.

Rose put her hands on her hips. "Where do you get off asking me what I do, Billy Bonney?"

"I'm sorry, Rose," he apologized. "I tell you Garrett has me on edge."

"Take your clothes off and climb on the bed," she said. "I'll sit up and wake you before dawn."

"You ain't in a mood to share the bed?" he asked cautiously.

"I said for you to get some sleep." She suppressed a smile. "Tired as you are... besides you never are much of a lover when you're tired like this."

"Hey!" he said defensively.

"Get some sleep. We'll see about it before you leave." She shook her head. Why did she always feel so obligated to the wild boy who called himself Billy the Kid? There was no logical answer, she just kept a special place in her heart for the carefree gunman.

She stood by the window and stared at the ghostly white mountainside which was studded with Spanish bayonet. Billy was already asleep, she noted, as his troubled breathing turned to snores. Just like a man to fall asleep when his head hit the pillow. She slowly shook her head in disbelief. Every lawman in the New Mexico

Territory wanted her guest and he was sleeping like a baby in her bed.

Rose awoke with a start. Exhausted, she had fallen asleep with her head on the table. It was light outside. Her whole body trembled in fear, she had overslept. Shakily, she pushed herself up, then tugged up her dress. Reality returned to her as she viewed the face-down, slumbering Billy in the bed. Sunlight shafted in the window on him. His one-piece underwear was wash worn and faded. She rushed to wake him.

He certainly was not a very big man for all the trouble he caused, she decided as she shook his shoulder. He was hardly more than a boy even if he tried to pass himself off as older than he was. She always considered his pretense at being a bad man, was a poor facade. Billy was just one of those men that never would grow up.

"I'm getting up," he said, looking at her through sleepy eyes. "What's wrong?"

"I dozed off," she said. "It's daylight and too late for you to leave." She straightened up, sweeping back her thick hair from her face. She felt full of regret for falling asleep.

He would have to stay all day at her place. Then the notion of Reagan's coming struck her. What would she do? She must think of something. She closed her eyes to consider their dilemma.

"What time is it?" he asked, sitting up.

"How should I know? I don't have a clock."

He was out of bed, pressing his face to the window to see. "What have you done?" He whirled on his heel and gave her a frown.

"I fell asleep," she said, holding out her palms."

"When's this marshal coming?"

"I'm not sure," she said.

He began dressing. "This is just great."

"Where are you going?" she asked.

"To get the hell out of here." He stood up and buckled on his gun belt.

"Someone will surely see you and have a posse on your tail. Sit down. We'll think this out."

"What do you recommend?" he asked, remembering to button his fly.

"There's room under the bed for you to hide," she said. "I can handle him. I just don't want either of you shot. Do you understand me, Billy Bonney?"

"You like him that much?"

She shook her head in anger. "I like you too. I want your word, Billy."

"Okay," he said with a downcast look. "I promise. But will this work?"

"Men are my business. You just get ready to get under my bed, savvy?'

Rose's head cocked at the sound of a shod horse coming up the hill. She whirled to face him. "Get out of sight."

He gathered his things and scrambled under the bed. As he wiggled out of sight, she drew a deep breath and touched her hair. She must look a mess. Oh well, Reagan probably wouldn't notice. She wet her lips, just so he didn't detect Billy.

She opened the door and smiled at the lawman as he hitched his horse to the front picket fence. He removed his hat and smoothed down his black hair. Reagan searched around before he came up the short walk.

"Morning, Rose," he said with a wide grin.

"You came early enough," she said and let him by, taking his hat. She knew Reagan wasn't a man to be backward around women. He quickly took her in his arms and began to kiss her. His deep hungry kisses made Rose grateful for his eagerness. The quicker their business was over, the sooner Reagan could leave. She would think of something when he was through and send him on his way.

Reagan was a lanky man. His skin paler than the starched shirt she unbuttoned for him. He hardly had a hair on his thin chest. Rose ran her hands over his skin and the corduroy ribs. He needed feeding, too.

His mouth was demanding on hers as she undid his belt buckle between them. Reagan's fingers were fumbling with the hooks and eyes hooks and eyes down the back of her dress. She eased from his hold to do that herself, fearful he might rip the dress open in his haste.

Deliberately, she let the dress fall, exposing her breasts. Rose knew from his look what the sight of them did for him.

She stepped out of the garment and put it on the chair, he was hurriedly shoving off her petticoats like a man on fire. Mildly amused at how viewing her body could move a man, she smiled as he eased her back on the bed. The wanton look in his dark eyes, told her enough as she laid on her back fearful of crushing poor Billy. What a mess.

"My God, Rose, why don't you live with me?"

To silence him, she pulled his face to hers and sealed his lips shut with a demanding kiss.

After their love making, Reagan slowly dressed. He sat in the wooden chair and pulled on his left boot. "They say you and Billy, the Kid once had a thing going between you?" he asked, in his Georgia drawl.

"Once," she replied, wrapping herself in a filmy duster. She dared not look back at the bed. "But he's gone."

"If you're over him, why don't you come live with me?"

"Reagan, you've asked me that before."

"Well?" He struggled to pull on the other boot. "Just think on it some more before you say no again."

"I will," she said sharper than she intended. Oh, God, why didn't he hurry and leave?

"Be a lot easier than what you're doing," Reagan offered.

"I promise I'll think on it. Now let me get some rest."

He looked over at the tossed bed covers and smiled. "We could both sleep together for a few hours?"

"No!" she said, herding him to the door.

"I think you're still stuck on Billy," Reagan argued as he took her in his arms. When he kissed her, she closed her eyes. Would he never leave?

He released her and headed for his horse. "You think on my offer, Rose."

"I will," she said and forced a smile for him.

She nearly collapsed against the door facing as the tall Georgian rode off down Cabbage Hill. Her breath came in small gulps as she waved a last time at the marshal. Light headed, she went back inside.

"You can come out now," she said, dropping heavily on a chair. She buried her face in her arms on the tabletop.

"Whew," Billy said, edging out on his back. "It was getting hot under there." He sat up and swept back his too-long, brown hair from his face. Then he grinned at her like a schoolboy ready to challenge her with some secret.

He laughed aloud as he pushed himself up. "That's close as I been to a lawman since I ran head on into a deputy in Tularosa one day."

"It isn't funny," she said.

"It was for me. You making love to him, just that far from me." Billy held his forefinger and second one about two inches apart.

"I've got to get out of this place," she said, standing up. Upset, she began to pace the floor.

"Where are you going to go?"

"Arizona, I don't know." She shook her head. "I need to go somewhere I don't know lawmen or outlaws. Anyway, the mines are nearly played out."

"Aw, I'd miss coming to see you." He put his arms around her and hugged her from behind her back.

"Billy, you wouldn't miss any woman," she said as he nuzzled her neck. "Besides, it's dangerous knowing you these days."

"Garrett?" he asked in her ear. "Are you scared of him?"

"That stiff shirt?" she asked in disgust, recalling the straight-backed sheriff. "I mean everyone is looking for you."

"They won't get me," Billy said, his chin on her shoulder as he rocked her from side to side.

"Why don't you stay in old Mexico?" she asked, irritated at his uncaring attitude.

"I ain't Mexican. That's why." He turned her around and kissed her.

Rose twisted her face free, resolved to give him her advice. "You'd be a damn sight safer there."

"Aw, Rose. I still got lots of friends. When they get in office, they'll pardon me."

She shook her head. Billy would never grow up. She was wasting her time. Why did he make her feel so sad when there was nothing she could do to change the course of his life or their relationship? "They better hurry and have the elections."

"Quit worrying, I've lived this long." His mouth closed off her protests. His kisses were more ardent than ever before. She felt him pulling her to the bed. Rose knew there was no use to argue about either his future, or intentions at the moment. He opened her thin duster, and slipped it off her bare shoulders. Rose wished she could stop him and clean up.

But in a moment, Billy's hot breath and tongue fed on her neck as he stoked the fires inside her. Never, could she recall him being so forcefully successful in arousing her. She pressed herself against him, wishing for more.

Soon her breath came in short clutches. But Bill did not stop kissing, teasing and fondling her. Delirious with his stimulation, she arched her back in expectation. Her hips ached to receive him.

When he finally entered her, she felt removed from Cabbage Hill, on a cloud floating over green farmland. Not in the desert, making wild love to a renegade cowboy. So intoxicated with ecstasy, they thrust hard to reach another plateau. She even worried the bed might crash.

Billy was the stallion she always dreamed about. The prince that existed in storybooks and then only for princesses. Never had she soared so high over and over again. Their sweat-slick bodies squeezed out the last drop of passion in their loins

Exhausted, they just lay in each other's arms, neither ready to speak. Rose became choked up, realizing he would soon be gone. Her heart ached as she clung to him. Any minute tears could leak from the corners of her eyes.

"Don't worry so much," he said, raising up on his elbow. "I still got more lives to lead."

She shook her head, a sour lump gathered behind her tongue. A sharp pain in her chest felt like an arrow had pierced her heart. And all this grief and worry, she mused, for a boy outlaw.

"Was I that bad this time?" he asked, a wide grin exposed his prominent front teeth. She buried her face on his bare shoulder.

"No," she sobbed, "You were the best lover I've ever had."

"Come on, Rose, quit your damned crying," he said.

She didn't dare speak. Why did she feel this was the last intimate moment she would ever spend with Billy? She felt powerless to change the matter.

Later, she trimmed his hair. He needed to look nicer, like someone cared about him. Rose even found some buttons for his threadbare suit coat. She dismissed the idea of doing more than sewing on the buttons. The day wore on congenially.

The sun dropped and Billy stood up as though he couldn't wait much longer to leave.

"Best you don't know where I'm headed," Billy said as he held her by the shoulders. "Not that I don't trust you, but you won't have to lie to them."

She agreed.

"Aw, a friend of mine has a ranch, I can stay there. Ol' Garrett won't find me," he said. "Cross my heart."

"Billy, why don't you go back..." His fingers silenced her lips as he gathered her in his arms.

"Rose. Don't fret about me. Why, in a couple weeks I'll circle back like I always do." Then he kissed her goodbye. Rose chewed on her lower lip as she watched his dark figure run for the arroyo in the twilight with the too long coat sleeves and the weather-beaten, high crown hat. Where had he left his horse? Some *companero* had kept it for him. Billy had plenty of amigos.

A week later, making her nightly rounds, Rose slipped in the doors of the Silver Moon Saloon. She halted at the sight of all the men cloistered at the bar. What were they celebrating?

"Hey! Rose!" A miner raised his mug high, sloshing some suds over the lip. "Here's to Pat Garrett! He gunned down that damned Billy the Kid!"

Thunderstruck by the news, Rose felt the blood drain from her face. She lurched between two men so she could reach the bar for support. Dazed for a moment, she focused and refocused her eyes at her own pale image in the mirror behind the bar. No, she wouldn't pass out. The nausea rose in her throat.

"Are you all right, Rose?" Duffy asked.

"I'm fine," she said as her composure returned.

"He shot that Billy Bonney three times," a drunk said, inches from her face.

She pushed the man away. Duffy was calling to her as she blindly rushed through the bat wing doors. On the boardwalk in front she gripped a post for support.

Billy was gone. He was never coming back. The carefree young man who had stolen her heart and broken it so many times—was dead. Rose shook her head. She had known all the time he would never be taken alive. That stiff-backed, bastard Garrett—she wished him in hell.

The cool night air drove out her self-pity and grief. Billy Bonney was dead. Nothing she could do would bring him back. Not one damn thing. All the nights she worried and cried for him—it was over.

She patted her hair, hitched up the front of her dress and set out with her skirts in hand. Billy would have expected her to do it like this. The easygoing fool... she set out to find the night Marshal, John Reagan. Rose planned to have him ask her to move in.

Passage by Starlight

The stage run to Coyote Springs took eight hours. That time frame included the thirty-minute layover at Cyrus Vance's stage stop to change the horses, empty your bladder and eat some of his burnt red beans. Cyrus's half Navajo wife always managed to scorch the frijoles before she slopped them out on tin plates to the passengers and the Hawkins and Hawkins stage drivers like me.

"You're running late," old Cyrus commented as he scooted in beside me at the driver's table.

"Yeah, they run a wheel off coming from Tombstone to Benson," I offered between wolfed down spoons of bitter beans. "It means I have to go over the grade after dark, too."

The notion *after dark* eating at my guts didn't bother the old man, he was more interested in something else in the room. The stage run over those Friscos with all those renegades off the reservation wasn't my idea of a Sunday school picnic. I could tell what had his attention; he was watching the lady passenger from Tombstone. The corner of his mouth finally turned up in lurid pleasure under his unkempt pepper colored beard. "Who is she?"

"Her name is Mary Logan according to the last driver," I said dryly. Then I washed the over cooked taste down with some strong black coffee.

"She's sure a looker," he said with a rue filled shake of his head. His rummy eyes held fast on the black tressed woman. She stood by the doorway in the red light of sundown. No doubt, she had not wanted any portion of Cyrus's squaw's concoction in her delicate stomach.

I studied her through the vapors of my second cup of coffee. The blue dress she wore was expensive; no doubt she came from wealth. Her slender jaw, almost hollow cheeks and sleepy eyes fascinated me. A bachelor of thirty, on my pay, I could never consider such a woman, except for a few moments in my daydreams.

"Them horses are ready," Cyrus said as he clapped me on the shoulder.

"Those half broke ones hitched in the back?" I asked, not trusting his help. Hawkins and Hawkins had a few green teams that they'd worked into the system. I'd driven them the week before and had hoped Charlie Dickens had taken them back to Benson on his turn. They needed lots of driving and training.

"How late will we be getting to Coyote Springs?" The fancy dressed passenger in the Prince Albert coat demanded right up in my face. I noted his tone of sarcasm and impatience.

"I expect we'll get there before midnight," I told him. Ignoring his overbearing ways, I pushed past him.

"The schedule says—"

"Doing the best we can. Get in the coach. We're leaving. If the Apaches don't get us, we'll be there by then." I realized my words were strong and I removed my hat for her when I turned to face her. "Ma'am, the ride from here on maybe a little rough."

"I understand." She smiled softly. An angel couldn't have sounded better. It made the dread I had for the ride ahead fly away like a Sonora dove's swift wings.

In his faded underwear top and stained britches, Cyrus came out to see us off. He waited until I had everyone loaded and the door shut before he spoke to me . "If'n that renegade Chee don't stick a feathered shaft in your back side, you ought to make some time with that looker."

I didn't bother to give him any satisfaction with a reply. Without a commend, I climbed on the seat. One fancy dan, a whisky drummer and her—four of us to get over those saw toothed mountains in this ship.

"See you next run, Cyrus!" And I kicked off the brake, shouted to the horses, working the reins in my hand and I wheeled them out of the station.

The sun had set, perhaps I had an hour of lingering twilight. The horses acted fresh and we made good time up the long grade to the top of Frisco Mountains, then the road leveled but we were hemmed in by the tall pines. No moon, only the stars to guide my way up the narrow cut that sliced the black trees. This land held many an Apache renegade. Even the word, Apache, made most folks hereabouts apprehensive. The hour was late and there were still several miles to cover in the darkness, the trip would be unduly long. My total concern was for the horses and coach— getting all of us there alive.

It must have been a bear that spooked them. Whatever it was, the lead team bolted aside and the green pair went berserk. The coach lurched sideways despite my desperate attempt to control the horses. The stage careened on two wheels—I knew it would spill as I sawed on the reins to right it. Too late to save it from turning over, I let go of the lines, jumped to clear the box and went air borne to land among some stiff pine boughs. The lynch pin broke and the terrified horses raced off into the night.

A fierce stab in my left side slowed me as I fought my way to my feet where the two upright wheels of the stage spun freely. Despite the fire in my side, probably from broken ribs, I was grateful there were no war cries slicing the night as I hurried to find out about my passengers' condition. "Get us out of here!" the fancy one demanded.

I scrambled up the ribbed underside of the coach and with some effort jerked open the door. "I'm trying. Here give me your arms," I said, seeing her hat.

With a little strain, I hoisted her out until she was seated on the door facing. "Are you all right?" I asked.

"I think so," she said softly. She adjusted her hat and I thought she smiled pleasantly at me.

"The rest of you all right in there?" I asked.

"No. How long will it take to get this coach on all four wheels and on our way?"

I frowned at the man's impatience as I struggled to help him out. My side shot full of pain and his awkwardness combined to make me strain until he finally bellied out on the side of the coach.

"I have to be in St John's by seven in the morning," he said.

I looked at him in disbelief, shook my head and then reached down to help the drummer, who did most of the escaping by himself. The peddler out, I eased down on the ground, grateful no one had been seriously hurt in the accident.

"Wait Miss, one of us will help you," I said straightening up and seeing her intent.

"What are you waiting for?" the man demanded from a top the stage.

"Mister, those horses are half way to Coyote Springs," I said as I swung her down on her feet. My heart almost ran away with itself, me having hold of the ribs of the woman's corset. I didn't want to let go, but for the sake of decency I did.

"I demand you do something!"

"Ah hell Kyle," the whisky drummer said as he climbed down. "Don't make such a pompous ass out of yourself. Ain't none of us hurt. Damned lucky ain't we, lad?"

"Yes, we are. I'll start a fire," I said for her benefit. The mountain night air had a chill. We were twice as lucky it hadn't been an Indian raid, but I saw no reason to mention that and upset her.

"A fire would be nice," she said.

"Fire? No, you don't. Set out this instant and get us some transportation!" Kyle ordered as he climbed down. "I have to be in St John's to catch that train in the morning."

I didn't bother to answer him. It was near twelve miles to Coyote Springs and I had no notions of setting out a foot in the dark for there. Beside Jim Severs would send a buckboard up for us when those horses came screaming in without a coach. He'd be along before daybreak.

"That Kyle is something else," the drummer said under his breath joining me in a search for fuel.

"I couldn't help the wreck but he's about impossible to deal with." I glanced off in the dark, I could hear him blowing off steam about the sorry stage line

"I just dread hearing about it all night," the drummer lamented.

I agreed and started back with my arms full of wood. Kyle rushed up in my face,

"Aren't you going to do anything?"

"Gawdamighty Kyle," I swore at the pain in my ear his shouting caused. "I ain't deaf. If you're in such an all fired hurry, point those fancy shoes north. Coyote Springs is about a dozen miles up this road."

"No, I paid for my passage."

"If you think that I'm packing you on my back out of here, think again." My breath ragged through my nose as I knelt down and busied myself starting the fire. "Do something useful. Go find some dry wood. I promise you that help will be along directly."

My words silenced him. He took a few steps and stopped. "But it's dark out there."

"So?"

"I can't—see."

"That's the same reason I ain't taking off afoot myself," I said pointedly enough he could understand. The Lucifer match, I struck on my leg, flashed alive and I held it to the pine needles until they flared up. I saw her face in the blaze. The vision of her warmed me as much as any fire.

Kyle began cussing the stage line and everyone else as he stomped around like a spoiled child. His fresh tirade was uncalled for and I could see it embarrassed Mary Logan. If the drummer hadn't called him down first, I would have.

"That ain't no way to talk around a lady. Hush your cussing, Kyle."

"Go to hell, you two bit whiskey peddler. I'll cuss who ever and whenever I want. Why she ain't nothing but a slut."

In two steps, I had his lapels in my fists and jerked him to his tip toes. "Apologize to her this minute," I raged through my teeth.

"Apologize? Why she's just a Tombstone sporting woman—"

The words were barely out of his mouth when I drove a right uppercut to his chin. The blow set him on the ground. On his butt, his bowler hat spilled, he rubbed his jaw and acted disoriented.

"Get up! I aim to finish this man to man," I said putting up my dukes.

"Don't," she asked quietly pulling on my sleeve. "Mr. Kyle is merely upset by the unfortunate delay."

"Hell—I mean—he ain't got no call," I stuttered unsure of my words.

"He's right," she began, "I guess no one ever escapes their past." Her words saddened me so much that I nearly set out a foot for Coyote Springs. How could such a beautiful woman have been what he...

It was near dawn when Jim Severs and two of his men armed with rifles brought out the buckboard for us. Kyle must have caught a later train at St Johns; I never saw the whiskey drummer again. There are times to this day that I miss driving a stage; having those frisky horses four up. Mary and I ranch up here in Idaho. I guess I'll never drive another. Stagecoach driving ain't a good life for a man with a wife and family.

Centennial Hell-abration

Hotter than blazes and calendar wise, I figured it must be six days shy of the Fourth of July and the U. S. of A's centennial celebration. My plans were to be in Fort Laramie for all the hurrah and fire works, but I still had two hundred miles of Sioux Indian country to cross.

For two days, I'd been ducking dozens of Indian bands on the move. They acted like they were headed to all the points on a compass. That bothered me because they usually hunted buffalo in the Powder River country at this time of the year for their winter food supply. This vast region wedged between the Black Hills and the Rockies had the best hunting left.

Nothing like the surplus of game that there had been twenty years before when the Crows still claimed it. In that period, they hardly ever had to move camp, the game was so plentiful. But the past few days, I'd only seen small remnant groups of buffalo. But the Indians, I had observed from hiding, seemed more interested in moving away than in gathering food.

To avoid still another war party's approach, I set my grey horse down a steep sided ravine, the two packhorses on his heels. When I heard the first cry for help, I reined up the grey and cocked my Sharps.

A pregnant Sioux squaw lay on the side of the hill, I saw her motioning for me. Her warhorse lay dead, crumbled in a pile a few yards away. He showed several fresh wounds. Still hitched between travois poles, I decided, the animal must have fallen down the bank when he expired.

97

The hair bristled on the back of my neck. The country crawled with hostiles. My fingers tightened on the stock of my .50 caliber Sharps. Suspicious of a trap, I searched around for signs of an enemy. She looked too much like a decoy to lure me off guard.

The woman acted desperate for help. She kept shaking her head as if my concerns were unneeded and urgently waved for me to come help her. The two bloody stubs of her recent amputated fingers were obvious. They meant she was a widow. In her sorrow she'd cut them off and then drifted away from her band.

When I dismounted I saw her face was bathed in an oily sweat. She indicated her bloated bare belly.

The notion of what she expected of me, took me back for a moment. I'd gutted a million buffalo, wild game, once even ate a Pawnee buck's liver, but when it came to birthing a baby, I felt awful anxious. That was what her jabbering in Sioux was all about.

"Help me have my baby."

Filled with dread, I set aside the long gun. Then hoping I didn't get sick and puke, I forced down the knot behind my tongue. Meekly I examined between her brown legs. She looked about to have the thing; the sight of a circle of black skull relieved me.

"Strain!" I shouted at her. "Push girl."

She did. Then she gave a sharp scream with her efforts and his lubricated little face sloshed out. I cleared the membrane and mucous away. Before I could do any more, she pushed his shoulders and arms out into the world. To clear the little fellow's hips took an extreme effort from both of us. Him slicker than snot didn't help me either get him clear. But when he cried out loud, the little guy eased all my worries about him being alive.

Probed on her elbows, Cut Finger smiled as I knotted the umbilical cord. She made a biting sign. I hesitated. My knife would cut it—but at her insistence, I bit the cord in two. Relieved, she laid back down on the brown grass.

I handed her 'Slick' and she opened her blouse for him to nurse. A little pride swelled in me at our success. I hadn't done much to help but the little guy was here and hungry.

My work done, I wiped my sticky hands on the grass and started for the grey. Helping a poor defenseless squaw hadn't hurt me, but I was anxious to put some distance between me and these hostiles. Those bucks might not believe how good a mid wife I'd become, besides my scalp still felt good on my head.

"Wait," she said in Sioux. "I have no one. The Long Knifes killed my man two days ago. That was his horse that died."

"Did they attack your camp?" I asked.

"Yes and we killed all of them."

"A detail?" I asked, in disbelief. Indians might have killed a few soldiers wandering around, but she sounded like there were more than a few dead Blue Legs,

She struggled to try and sit up. *"Many Blue Pants dead."* She made a wide sweeping gesture to indicate the expanse of the dead ones. Her face fell. "So is *my man.*"

I was in a pickle barrel full of brine. How could I leave her to fight off wolves with that new boy and all? Don't no one ever think I ain't as mean as any ex-army scout that ever forked a horse. By damn, old General Phil Sheridan will testify to this day to that fact.

Indian squaws come tough. I figured she'd be ready to travel in twelve hours, but with all the bands passing that half day gave a greater chance of my being discovered. The next problem to solve; I needed to locate an extra horse for her and the baby to ride. That wouldn't be easy to find either, the Sioux kept their horse stock close to camp.

My grey nickered and I nearly fell over myself drawing my Army model Colt. A small fuzzy-brown mare with white saddle marks on her withers came down the draw toward my stock.

When I glanced over at her, Cut Finger smiled like she had expected it. Then she laid back on the grassy slope. The baby asleep on top of her. Those bare-pointed nipples wet with his slobbers, shone in the sun.

The needed horse had arrived. I tried not to be superstitious, but that mare's arrival spooked me.

Late that afternoon, Cut Finger bathed the boy with my canteen water and took a papoose board from her things in the packs on the dead horse.

After we ate some 'buff' jerky together, she mounted the mouse colored horse, I took the lead and we headed south by starlight.

July first, we hid from an approaching dust sign. A company of cavalry passed not a hundred yards from our hiding place. If I'd been a hostile, I could have shot the gold bars off that captain. A pair of lazy half breed scouts were leading him; they needed their butts kicked for not seeing me and the woman.

All my hurrying had a purpose. The way I figured, this country of mine only had one, one hundred year birthday. I'd planned all winter to be in Fort Laramie for the whing-ding on Independence Day. When we struck the North Plat, I considered leaving Cut Finger, the boy and galloping on ahead. But she took so much pride in herself and that baby, I just couldn't leave her.

The night before we reached Fort Laramie, she bathed in the river and beat our deerskins clean in corn meal A man should never abandon a prideful woman. A slovenly one ain't worth nothing but it's different about one with that much dignity.

I crossed the last rise, dressed in my best buckskins. She'd dug out an elk tooth necklace to wear; the necklace probably worth a Spencer rifle. Her raven hair was done in tight braids and eagle feathers trailing; we were a fine looking outfit going into Fort Laramie.

But as we approached, no one spoke to us or hardly looked our way; even the tame Injuns faded away instead of pestering and begging like they usually did. There was something out of place; I couldn't imagine what was wrong.

"Ain't this July Third, 1876?" 1 asked the first sergeant I rode up to on the grounds. "Where's the celebrating?"

"You ain't heard the news?"

"What news?"

"The hostiles wiped out the entire Seventh Cavalry including Colonel George Armstrong Custer and his entire command at the Little Bighorn."

I shook my head. "Not the entire Seventh?"

"Every blood letting son. There won't be much Centennial celebrating here, mister."

Grim faced, I agreed and rode on. For some reason I began whistling the "Garry Owens" tune. The past winter I'd stopped off and watched the Seventh Cavalry troopers drilling on Fort Abraham Lincoln's parade ground. Their music always stuck with me.

Cut Finger rode up, put her hand on my arm and nodded. She remembered. *"Their song, those soldiers that died sang that too."*

On Eagle's Wings

The eagle soared. His powerful wingspan carried him on the updraft as his sharp eyes searched the fir clad slopes and open meadows beginning to green with spring's first grass. He swept down slope over the shaggy coated band of Indian ponies splashed in dun, red and bays. The herd ignored his flight as they eagerly cropped the new growth.

A young paint colt struggled to his feet, frightened by the huge bird's racing shadow. Awkward for a moment, the colt found his spring like legs and galloped around his pot bellied dam. Head high, his short mane unfurled, she listened as the youngster whined while he circled her. His voice mixed with the eagle's piercing screams.

Red Star, the Crow maiden, smiled at the eagle-horse activity as she waded from the icy stream. Beads of water glistened on her sleek tawny skin. She bent her head to the side to wring the moisture from her long black hair. Her heart beat fast from the cold bath, but the sun's warmth had begun to warm her slender body as she stood on the bank and admired the eagle's flight.

She was grateful the great spirit of the sky had returned. This was a good omen. But she could not afford the luxury of viewing him for long. She must quickly dress and get to her day's work. The grey snowy elk skin dress was almost finished. All she lacked were a few stitches and the trade beads to decorate the fringe. Why was the completion of this garment so important to her? She shook her head at the consuming obsession that had gripped her ever since the deep snows of winter when the dress's completion had became so necessary to her.

She stretched her arms to the sky. "Tell me, oh, great one, why do I toil so on a wedding gown when I have no man to marry?"

Disappointed at his sharp reply, Red Star dropped her head. She did not understand his words. As she began to dress, she wondered why none of her past suitors had ever pleased her. Several powerful tribesmen who had brought horses to her father's lodge, each time, Tall-Elk had accepted his daughter's negative response to the men's offer.

Her mother, Laughing-Woman had grown concerned. Younger girls were already married. Laughing Woman had pointed this out not understanding her daughter's hesitancy. Red Star recalled the words she had spoken at her mother's insistence that she find a man. They had mysteriously spilled from her lips in anger.

"My man will come for me on the back of an eagle." This speech was never formed by his conscious thinking. She felt taken aback and inwardly she was shocked at the implication that a spirit had used her tongue to tell the future.

"How long will you wait for this dream?" Laughing-Woman asked. "You will be past the age that men look for wives. And what if this eagle-rider does not come?"

Unshaken from her own convictions, Red Star held to her own belief that this prophecy would come true. The return of the strong wind walker screaming above her in the clear air confirmed her deepest belief—her man would come on the eagle's wings.

As she pulled on her leggings, she turned her ear to listen to a distant sound. The fresh morning air carried a faint, unknown song. Was it a sign of his impending arrival? Or simply the eagle's own anthem of return. She did not know. Dressed, she resigned herself to fate and ran lithely toward the camp. She passed the large Crow pony herd, which barely paused to eye her suspiciously.

Filled with anticipation, she was anxious to recheck the stitches in the wedding gown in time for his arrival.

"I must be ready," she panted. She spoke aloud, surprised at the shortness of her breath. "One day he will come for me.

High above the morning campfires smoke, the eagle used his powerful wings to go higher. His scope widening as he circled to gain altitude. To his keen ears, the soft clop of a pack train's hooves drew his attention.

A tall white man rode at the head of the column. In his four-point blanket jacket, he sat ramrod tall, well over six feet, crowned with a wide brimmed hat from a Philadelphia hatter's mold. In the crook of his arm, an oily Spencer repeating rifle gleamed in the sun. His pale blue eyes studied the land as the powerful gray stallion beneath him cat-hopped up the trail.

Under the well-trimmed blondish beard, his thin mouth was set in a straight line. A man of thirty winters, Karien McCollough was grateful the last one had passed. Too many nights, he had lain awake and listened to the wind's attempt to tell him something that he could not decipher. Perhaps being back on the trail and trading with the friendly tribes, he could drive this nagging force from his thoughts.

He twisted in the saddle to view Matthew Stone's red stocking cap as his assistant brought up the rear of the train. "That's a big eagle," Karien shouted.

Matthew raised his eyes for a view and nodded. "He's telling them that we're coming."

Rather than shout again, Karien hoisted his rifle aloft to indicate that he had heard the man.

This marked their third season together on the trail. Matthew was an ox of a man. Karien found him good company, neither a drunkard nor windy to excess.

As the trail wound skyward, Karien recalled the first time he had laid eyes on the former sea going Matthew who had been brawling with three post loafers at Fort Laramie. When they started with their knifes for the defiant Matthew, Karien had interceded by drawing his Colt and firing a shot at their feet.

"I'm grateful to you sir," Matthew had said. Rivulets of sweat mixed with the fort's dust streaked his clean shaven face.

"No need," Karien said as he reloaded his Colt. He was satisfied that the fleeing ruffians did not wish to tangle with both of them.

"Oh, indeed, sir. Allow me to buy you a mug of ale."

Karien was amused at the man's offer. "I doubt the sutler has any ale. Probably some kind of hell water he calls whiskey. But I accept your offer."

"Good." Matthew said as the two men introduced themselves and shook hands.

"Matthew, those loafers will bear watching," Karien said with a hard look back toward the lodges where the threesome had sulked off. "What brings a sea going man to this part of the Kansas Territory?"

They started across the open grassland between Squaw Town and Fort Laramie's Sutler post on the higher ground.

"I look sea going, huh?" Matthew asked.

"Pantaloons, knit shirt and stocking cap. Yes, you look fresh off a ship."

"Well, actually I'm looking for a new trade," Matthew said, easily matching Karien's long strides.

"Can you ride a horse?" Karien asked, glancing over at the broad shouldered man.

"I can ride him or carry him," Matthew said.

Karien smiled at the man's words. There was little doubt this husky seaman could shoulder up an Indian pony. That day began their partnership trading with the friendly tribes.

Karien halted the stallion at the crest to view the valley of the Crow's camp. A cool breath of wind swept his face as he studied the wide depression. A cloud of smoke hung around the lodge pole clusters of the many tepees.

This was the camp of Silver Bear. A messenger of the chief had brought word to Karien that his people would welcome his pack train in their camp. Karien raised his rifle as a signal to Matthew that he had located the village.

The stallion screamed as he scented the unfamiliar mares. His challenge echoed a dozen times across the vastness as Karien sent him down the path. A sharp heel to the horse's ribs urged him down the path. Confident the horse would not fall with him, Karien mused at how few men rode greater mounts. At Fort Lincoln, General George Custer with his stable full of expensive horses, had offered Karien an exorbitant price for Big Man. He'd respectfully declined the offer.

Rotten snow remained in the shade as Karien crossed the forested benches, he lost sight of the village, then it came in full view again when the trail broke out of the pungent groves of fir.

For some unknown reason this particular journey seemed destined since the onset, he had felt a pull of tension.

The French called the feeling he experienced deja vu. He had never been in this valley before, yet each twist in the trail seemed a revelation of a past journey.

The lightening scarred snag to his right... Karien blinked. Why did he possess such a deep-rooted memory of this route?

Unmoved by superstitious things, he scoffed at tales of ghosts and the supernatural yarns, but a small amount of dread gathered in the pit of his stomach, this was more than a coincidence. For a split-second, he held a vision of a Crow maiden in a white elk skin dress. When he closed his eyes—she was gone.

Was he going mad? He drew a deep breath of the thin air to settle himself. This whole matter had him on edge. Karien couldn't remember ever being this disturbed by the unknown before in his life.

He paused on a wide treeless flat to allow the horses to breath. Removing his hat, he combed his yellow hair with his fingers. Absorbed in his thoughts, Matthew's words barely penetrated his absence.

"...you all right, sir?"

"Oh." Then Karien nodded affirmatively. "I have had strange feelings about this place."

"Bad ones?" Matthew's full eyebrows hooded his deep set eyes.

"I'm not sure." Karien slipped out of the saddle and stretched his tall frame. "I'm just having doubts about this place we're headed for."

"Silver Bear isn't supposed to be hostile?"

"No." Karien leaned on his rifle barrel. "There is something down there. I'm just not sure."

Matthew dismounted and did a few deep knee bends in a frog like fashion. "I can't feel a thing about what's ahead."

"Good, last time we both had bad feelings we nearly rode into a Sioux war party."

"Cost us three pack horses," Matthew reminded him.

"A cheap price for our hair." Karien squinted to view the eagle's pass as the great bird swept over the valley. The bird's ear piercing challenge was answered by Big Man.

Both men grinned at the animal's defiance of the other.

"Big Man wants to argue with that bird," Karien said.

"Be a devil of a fight," Matthew offered.

Karien agreed with a nod. Did his horse even sense something wrong? The whole business was unsettling. Filled with a new resolve to go on, Karien gave a toss of his head to Matthew as a signal he was ready to ride.

"Sir?" Matthew asked as he grasped the Mexican saddle horn to remount.

"Yes."

"I'll be ready just in case we ride into a hornet's nest."

"I have no doubt you will," Karien said in appreciation for the man's assurance.

"I've never seen you so bothered before."

Karien shrugged. "I guess we'll learn about it in due time."

"Aye sir. Get up, you land lubbering grass eaters," Matthew shouted at the pack string to get them in line as they started off in the final flight down into the valley.

Karien drew a deep breath. Whatever was ahead wasn't far.

Restless, Red Star crossed and recrossed her feet as she reworked the stitches in the sleeve. Why, she scowled, must this dress be so perfect? Nothing pleased her; even her seamstress skills disappointed her.

"A white trader is coming," Laughing-Woman announced from outside the lodge's flap. "Maybe he will have the blue beads that you want for the dress."

Red Star rose and pushed the door of skin aside. "Would you trade for some?"

Laughing-Woman smiled and agreed. "I will trade some of our furs for the beads. Come out and see them coming"

"No, thank you," Red Star said and went back to her sewing. She stretched the leather taut to push the steel needle through. There was no time to go stare at some strange white eyes. Besides most white men looked too boldly at Indian women to suit her; she had found their stares discomforting as a girl when they lived near the army.

They were all boisterous, she mused, and loud. Most of them never bathed, she wrinkled her lip at the thought of the trader from two summers before who had offered her father a dozen Sioux horses for her.

Tall-Elk seeing the disappointment in his daughter's eyes had sent the hairy-faced man away. The white eye later took a young widow, Way-of-Walking for his wife. Red Star had worried for Way-of-Walking as she had rode out on the claybank mare as if she were a princess.

The young woman, Red Star mused, would find her lot with the white men far from royalty. The memory of that close encounter made her shudder with cold chills. Why did some Crow women think white men were so great? Let the wanton, dog eating, Dakota women have them. She had noticed a lot of Sioux women riding with traders.

The camp curs were yapping as Red Star finished the last stitch. She scrambled to her feet and pulled off the deerskin shirt over her head to try on the new one. The elk skin dress was finally complete except for the blue beads that she intended to string on the fringe.

The sunlight light shown through the translucent tent skins. Standing bare to her waist, she prepared to put on the new garment, when the shrill scream of the stallion made her pause. The animal must be powerful, she mused as an involuntary chill of fear ran up her back. She wanted to see it.

Red Star held the new dress to her breasts and went to the flap to peek at the horse. She caught sight of the silver stallion's dish face, small pin ears, and long flowing mane. His delicate nostrils flared as he distrustfully snorted at the camp smells and individuals.

From her discreet position, she could only see the rider's buckskin clad legs. She dropped to her knees, hoping to see the man's back after he passed by her.

To her shock, when she looked up, his gaze met her own. Cold as the color of silver coins, his eyes held her for a moment that seemed an eternity before she fell away to be out of his sight.

Shaken, she scrambled to her feet. She admonished herself for acting like a silly child, gawking at a white eyes. He must think she was daft or very bold. She folded her arms over her firm breasts—she had no intention of exposing herself again to him. Seeking absolution, Red Star raised her eyes to the top of the lodge. The Great Spirit must protect her for she had no intentions of becoming a squaw woman. The duration of his stay, she must remain out of his sight.

Karien felt awed. Who was the beautiful woman in the lodge doorway who looked so familiar? He slapped the stallion on the neck for snorting at the people. If Big Man kept acting up, the Indian women might become afraid of him and would not come to trade with them.

"Hello, great chief of the Crow," Karien shouted as the obvious headman came out in his full headdress. He stood at the end of the open lane of onlookers. Silver-Bear wore a trade blanket shawl and his braids were grey streaked. He made an imposing figure with several more sub-chiefs around him.

"Eyes of Sky," Chief Silver Bear said. "We have waited long for the yellow haired one to come and trade with our women."

"Your horses wintered well," Karien said, knowing that the Crow prized their herds and a compliment was always well accepted.

"If we had colts from that great horse of yours, we would smile." The chief's words drew several approving nods from his entourage.

"He is willing," Karien said as he dismounted. These Crows seemed a very open people. Perhaps all his concerns were unfounded. But where was the woman? He looked over the crowd; there was no sign of her.

"Come Eyes-of-Sky," Silver-Bear said, holding the tepee flap back for him to enter. "We will smoke to our friendship."

Karien raised his rifle, without turning, in a signal for Matthew to watch the stock. Then he bent low to enter the council's chamber. His eyes adjusted to the dim light as he took the place indicated by the chief.

He waited as the pipe bearer filled the ornate long stemmed pipe. The words of the others were low. Karien was accustomed to being the object of stares at such meetings for it happened in most all the camps where he stopped.

After the pipe smoking ceremony, Karien emerged and motioned for Matthew who was guarding the pack train from the crowd of giggling, inquisitive women.

"We better set up down stream," Karien said, taking Big Man's reins from the youth holding him. "These ladies look ready to do business with us."

As he swung his leg over the saddle, he felt disappointed. She was not among the crowd.

"Who are you looking for?" Matthew asked, riding up beside him with the horses in tow.

"Was I that obvious?" Karien asked as he smiled toward the large gathering of happy, chattering women who were going along with them.

"You've been searching for someone or thing ever since we came in here," Matthew said. "I know that look, sir."

"She isn't here," Karien said.

"Who isn't here?"

"Never mind, I'll point her out if I ever see her again."

"Oh, Lord," Matthew said. "I've never seen you worry about any woman, let alone a Crow."

"There have been stranger things," Karien said, with an edge of irritation. "Let's get to work or haven't you noticed the crowd we've attracted?"

"Aye, sir," Matthew said, with a wave of his hand.

Karien returned Matthew's salute with a scowl. Karien mused about his military service; grateful that was far behind him. Matthew still teased him about his role as captain in the cavalry. The man's knowledge of Karien's rank had led to all the sirs.

Their blankets and goods spread on the ground, Karien dropped to his knees ready to trade. The women pushed in closer, ohing and ahing as he took out goods to show them.

He made a sign that he was ready for a customer. A round-faced older woman, her arms loaded with furs, pushed her way to the front. When she dropped on her knees to face him, she showed him her broken tooth smile.

"You got plenty goods?" she asked as she spread out her pelts of otter, fox and lynx.

"Plenty," Karien said.

The woman took a kettle, beads, a comb and some red yard goods material in trade. So the trading began and stretched through the day. His piles of furs grew and the pannier's supplies went down.

In the lodge, wearing her old dress, Red Star was sullen, still angry with her own exposition.

Laughing-Woman entered and spoke to her, "Let us go trade for those beads and some material."

"No."

Her mother frowned. "Why not? This is the one they call Eyes-of-Sky, the trader that Chief Silver Bear sent for because of his good dealings with other people."

"I am going to remain here," Red Star stated, unmoved because some yellow haired white man was in their camp. "Go see him, yourself."

"Are you afraid of him?"

"No. I fear no white man."

Laughing-Woman frowned. "He is a good one to fear. Very tall and handsome. Is that why you won't go with me?"

"I do not want anything to do with him."

"You don't want any man," her mother said and shook her head. "Besides he probably has a woman. He could have whoever he wants."

"Not me," Red Star snapped.

"I'll go trade for your beads," her mother said and began gathering some of the furs they had worked up during the winter.

She saw her mother's disapproving glance back as she departed the lodge. No matter, she was not going to allow him to see her again.

When Laughing-Woman knelt on the blanket before him, Karien saw the woman's resemblance to the maiden.

"You have blue beads?" she asked.

"Yes," he said, noting her clear English. "You speak the words of the white man well."

"My husband, Tall-Elk was a scout for your army. I learned it from him."

"Do you have a younger sister?" he asked, pouring the beads on the blanket for her to chose.

"Sister?" She blinked at his question.

"Never mind," he said wishing he had not asked her.

"How much for this many?" she asked, with her palm nearly full.

"Two fox," he said absently, becoming upset by the woman's presence. Karien knew the price was too cheap. After putting the precious glass beads in her pouch, Laughing-Woman quickly handed him two pelts as if she feared he might raise the price. Then she excused herself.

Karien tried to see where she went but she disappeared beyond the waiting throng. He regretted not seeing which lodge she went to. His next customer, a coy smiling girl hardly out of her teens, knelt down on the blanket. She laid down no furs so he wondered what she wished to trade. When he nodded, she opened her blouse and bared her breasts. Her hand reached for his, but not quick enough. Karien was familiar with such tricks and leaned back with his arms folded.

"No! Trade goods for furs," he said sharply, making signs with his hands that she could understand.

She smiled big, and rose while adjusting her blouse. Then she proudly walked away as the other women snickered over her attempted commerce. When she was gone, Karien rose to his feet and signaled to Matthew to come and barter with them for a while.

When they were through with the last customer, the sun was flaming down in a wedge between two peaks. Both men were exhausted.

"There's one in every camp," Matthew said.

"What do you mean?" Karien asked.

"A woman willing to trade her body for some trinkets."

"She was probably the most honest one here," Karien said. "I should have given her a red scarf, but I was afraid she'd come back later."

Matthew, busy unfurling the tent, said something inaudible. Karien guessed at the meaning of his partner's words.

"On your own time," he said, "you can go trade her a red scarf for a favor."

"Aye, sir."

"Let's get this thing up, I'm starving."

"A man makes a fortune in prime pelts and he's worried about eating," Matthew muttered, pushing the center poles into place.

"We will be busier tomorrow, those women were just testing our honesty today," Karien warned.

"I know, they'll figure we ain't crooks and come back for what they really need."

The tent finally set up, they moved their saddle and panniers inside the shelter against thievery. Then they sat outside on the ground in the twilight and chewed on buffalo jerky.

As deeper shadows engulfed the canyon, Karien watched the glow of the many cooking fires around the camp. The coffee water boiled on Matthew's small blaze.

"Hey, McCollough," Matthew said between hard bites on the jerky. "Weren't you married once? To a white woman I mean."

"Yes. She died while I was a lieutenant stationed in Minnesota." "Sorry, sir," the man said regretfully as he raised on his haunches to pour their coffee.

"No need, that was a long time ago."

Matthew glanced back. "You ain't exactly the squaw man type."

"I can't exactly see some fine educated lady either putting up with the likes of me."

"Aye, but an Indian wife has a different meaning at a place like say Saint Louis."

Karien nodded as he blew on his coffee. An Indian wife meant cutting ties with civilization. Fort Laramie maybe, the gold rush up on Cherry Creek but he couldn't ever go back to Ohio with one. He had only been there once since Sherry had died and that was in respect to her people to explain how their daughter had succumbed to cholera.

"Did you ever see this Crow woman again?" Matthew asked.

"No. But I think her sister came and traded for some blue beads this afternoon."

"But you never saw her before today?" Matthew sounded confused by the matter.

"A vision of her has been haunting me for a long time," Karien said pulling the kerchief from his neck to hold the hot cup.

"Maybe she's a witch?" Matthew asked.

"Aw, Matthew," Karien scoffed, "there are no such things."

"Aye, in England they got witches."

Karien shook his head. "She's very real. I saw her today."

"Oh, sir, I ain't doubting your keen eyes."

The coffee tasted good and seemed to revive him. "Today has been a long day. Tomorrow, I will go ask Silver Bear where she is."

"You are serious."

"Let's say I'm going to settle this." Karien sipped on his coffee and studied the spray of stars in the slice of sky between the two mountain ranges. He rolled his bottom lip against the sharp edge of his top teeth and tested his bristled lip. Whoever she was, she couldn't be very far.

Somewhere high on the mountain, a timber wolf howled. His throaty complaint seemed to plead with the night. Big Man answered, his shrill whistle and screams echoed as he stomped around on his short tether to the stout lodge pole pine.

In the lodge, unable to sleep, Red Star lay under her robes. Cold perspiration ran down her temples. She could hear the great horse's screams. She shuddered, then threw the covers back and scrubbed her face with her palms.

Where was this man with eyes like the sky? Red Star found herself inexplicably trembling.

Spellbound, she rose as if in a trance and put on her new dress. Silently, she slipped from the lodge. In the cool night air, she paused and located the low voices of the men talking in council and moved into the shadows to avoid them. She worked her way around the camp, her footsteps quiet on the blanket of needles.

Her heart beat faster in her throat as she approached the area of the traders. The big horse still screamed. Was he warning the man?

Cautiously, she approached him as he fretted on the short lead rope. The silvery light of the stars made his glossy coat shine. She blinked in amazement at the match of her dress and the horse's color. He continued to snort and paw as she neared him

Red Star held out her hand and spoke softly in the ways of horses. At first, he blew at her but fearless she advanced, his impatience seemed to melt when she touched his soft muzzle. He stood very still as she moved her palms over his nostrils to acquaint him with her smell.

She spoke to him in Crow as she stroked the long, wavy locks of his mane.

"Are you trying to steal my horse?" Karien asked softly from behind her.

She whirled at his words, ready to flee. Speechless, she stood with her back to the stallion and faced the trader they called Eyes-of-Sky. Her heart pounded so hard it knifed her. She found herself trembling with anticipation.

"Is it my horse that you want?" he asked.

When she did not answer, Karien stepped forward and grasped her arms. If she only wanted his horse—anger surged through him as he considered all the times he had wondered about her—for what? A simple horse thief. No, there was more than that to this long awaited meeting. Still, he cautioned himself not to expect too much.

"Who are you anyway?" he demanded, ready to shake an answer from her.

"I am the daughter of Tall-Elk, my name is Red Star," she said struggling loose from his hold. "And who are you to come to *my village* and spoil *my life*?"

"You have been ruining my life for months," he said and let her go.

She shook her head. Her English was so limited that she could not understand his meaning. She turned to leave.

"Wait!" he ordered. "Are you a spirit?"

"Red Star," she said, turning back to see him in the dim light.

"Are you a spirit?" he asked.

"No." She wondered why he disliked her so. Her arms burned where he had held her as if an eagle's talons had pierced through the skin. The notion froze her feet in place as she began to realize why she had come there. Not for the horse, but for him.

"Why did you hide from me?" Karien asked.

"I was afraid of you," she said. Where did her words come from? Had she spoken her own speech or that of a spirit.

"I'm pleased that you came here," he said and slowly took her in his arms. "I feared you were married. That you belonged to someone else."

"I belong to no man," she said more sharply than she intended.

This time his arms were gentle as he hugged her to his chest. When he smelled her clean hair, he felt the dread in his heart subside. All these years, he had been searching for something. Under the snow-capped peaks of the Big Horns, he'd found her.

She knew in her heart as she pressed her forehead against the fringe and beads of his leather shirt that this was to be her man.

Charlie's Last Gal

The town was deserted. A dozen stores and businesses were boarded up. Russian thistle piled on the porches and several of the dilapidated boardwalks had fallen into a dangerous state of disrepair.

Lacey shook his head in disbelief. What had happened to this place? Back in '83, this had been the hub of commerce. No less than a dozen saloons had been open twenty-four hours a day. A steady stream of customers had milled in the street night and day. The air punctuated with pistol shots, raucous laughter and screaming saloon women all over the place and twelve pianos, all tinkling a different tune. Freight wagons, oxen and mule teams, packhorses and buggies had congested this street in those days.

Lacey reined in his dun, noting that at least one place was still open for business. The name on the saloon, The Lucky Dame, was barely legible on the false front. The paint was so cracked and sun bleached, it was hard to tell it had once been dark green.

Stiff from the long ride, he dismounted and put the stirrup over the seat to undo the *latigos*. The cinch loosened, he cast a speculative look at the cracked front window. The town had sure gone downhill. He drew a deep breath and shoved his shirttail into his pants.

What made him hesitate about going inside? He had wanted a beer ever since he had crossed over the divide. His mouth watering for the first glass. He inhaled deeply, chiding himself for his reluctance. There wasn't a grizzly bear beyond those louvered doors unless it was stuffed.

Still wary, he searched the street again. Not a soul in sight. Damn, where had everyone gone?

He pushed through the batwing doors and entered the sour smelling saloon. His eyes adjusting to the darkened interior.

"Hello, stranger," a woman offered from behind the bar.

"Howdy," he acknowledged her greeting. Undecided, he stood wondering whether to sit at a table or stand at the bar. He chose the latter, strode over to it then placed his dusty boot on the brass rail at the base.

"What'll it be?" she asked.

He studied her for a moment. She was nice looking, possibly thirty years old; her light brown hair was clean and tied back. She wore a man's shirt that molded her breasts. It was unbuttoned just enough to expose the shadowy V of her cleavage.

"Guess I'll have a beer," he said. When she turned to draw it, he looked around. His gaze was drawn to the painting of the nude over the counter. A voluptuous model reclined on a mound of pillows. The artist had depicted her almost life-size.

"Some picture, ain't it?" the woman bartender asked, delivering the beer, the foam sliding down the side of the mug.

He felt a little uncomfortable talking to someone of the opposite sex about a painting of a naked lady. He cleared his throat and mumbled in agreement.

She turned her back to him and studied the picture. "I reckon to a man, she's real pretty," she commented in a detached voice. "But she seems a might padded to me. What do you say?"

"Yeah," he murmured, wishing he had taken his beer to a table. Restless, he shifted his weight and studied the suds in his glass.

The woman turned and cocked her head to look at him. "How old are you?" she asked abruptly.

He frowned at her. "Forty-six or close to it."

"That's what I figured. You've seen a few women without their clothes on in your time. Well, don't you think that one there is a little on the plump side?"

"Maybe," he said, his tone non-committed. Then he raised his mug, hoping to somehow escape her further questioning on the subject of the woman's shape.

"You're a stranger around here?"

"I've been gone a long time. Town seems to have died," he said, glad to change the conversation to another subject.

"Yeah, reckon it has. I was born here. Guess I'll dry up and die here."

"You own this place?" he asked hoarsely, the cold beer having slid down his throat like a chip of ice over a hot stove.

"Yes, all by myself." She nodded slowly. "My husband's dead."

"Sorry."

"Ain't no reason to be. He never did anything around here." She slapped the bar with her palm. "He got drunk and broke his neck. Happened right across the street. It was the night they had the last hurrah and closed down the whore house. Yeah, James fell down those stairs and never lived to tell about it," she said in a low voice.

He gazed out the window at the staircase alongside the boarded-up house of ill repute, then took another drink of his beer. It washed a bucketful of trail dust down his throat.

"Where did everyone go?" he asked, sneaking a glance at the artwork from the corner of his eye. He had to admit, the artist's model was a little on the fleshy side.

She ignored his question and followed his gaze with her own. "A gal wanted to buy that painting," she said.

"Huh?"

"My naked lady. A gal, who couldn't have been more than a teenager, came storming in here. She went behind the bar like she owned this place, looked at the buffalo skull in the corner of the painting and offered to buy her."

He squinted, trying to see the artist's signature. The light wasn't very good in the saloon and his eyes weren't what they use to be.

She gestured with her hand. "Come around here and take a closer look if you like."

He shook his head. "That's all right."

"You ready for another beer?"

"Sure." He handed her his empty mug.

"Well," she continued as she drew a fresh glass of beer, "that gal offered me quite a bit of money for the painting."

"She did?"

"Yeah, a lot more money than I'll make in the next ten years running this place."

"Oh?" He took the second beer and sipped on the foam.

"You'll never guess who she was?"

"No, I reckon I won't," he lied, having already guessed who the would-be-buyer was.

"She was the artist's wife," the woman said, leaning toward him as if telling him a secret.

"That right?" He turned sideways and glanced around. "Where is everyone?" he asked, wanting to change the subject of the rendition of womanhood on the wall. Besides he was having a difficult time keeping his eyes off both her and the painting.

"Who?"

"The townspeople," he said, turning back to face her. "This was a busy place, really booming back in '83."

"The mine played out." She shrugged. "There was a couple bad winters, froze out the cattle. When the railroad laid their lines south along the river—this place just sort of died."

"Why do you stay?" he asked curiously.

"Oh, I have a little business. Lord, I'm the only saloon in town. Saturday, some of the old hands come in. We wind up the that player piano and dance. What else could I do?"

"Nothing, I guess," he said debating whether to tell her the truth about the painting.

"I told that woman if I sold her that painting, there wouldn't be anything to bring them old bachelors in here. She's their woman, you know. My lady up there, keeps them happy. There ain't a house of ill-repute within a hundred miles."

"Yes," he said, feeling his face heat up with embarrassment.

"So, she's my shady lady. They line up and gawk at her. Kind of like you're doing," she added with a small laugh.

"What gives you your gall, girl?" He glared at her. She laughed again, but it was not a mocking laugh, more one of gentle amusement. She knew what her lady did for a man.

"Why she's what every man wants, voluptuous, wanton, waiting for him," she said.

Lacey drank more of his beer. Bad as he hated to admit it, the woman was right. Obviously, she knew a lot about men.

"The artist's wife hasn't been back to buy the painting?" he asked.

The woman snorted. "I ain't selling it!"

Lacey titled his head and peered openly at the painting. "Not even for two-thousand dollars?"

"Hell, she never offered me that much."

"I just wondered." He was beginning to enjoy himself. He openly studied her rounded full breasts and the gentle swell of her bare belly. He couldn't recall any woman in his life that well proportioned.

"Say, Mister, would you pay that much for her?"

Lacey blinked at the woman. "Hell, do I look like I have that much money?" He laughed, feeling a lot friendlier with the two beers inside him.

"Do you know something about my lady that I don't?" the woman asked.

"I just might. Let me come back there and get a good look at the signature," Lacey said. He went toward the end of the bar. She lifted the flat, hinged counter portion and allowed him past her.

He headed for the painting, trying not to stare too brazenly at the figure. His eyes squinted, he lowered his head and studied the buffalo skull. He finally nodded. "I thought it was his work."

"Why would anyone in their right mind pay two-thousand dollars for a nude painting?" she demanded.

"Respectability," Lacey said curtly as he walked back around the counter.

"How's that?" The woman looked at him with hard eyes.

"She's bought up every nude he ever painted, except this one."

The woman walked briskly toward the cash register. "I've got her address right here." Holding up a card, she read it aloud, "Great Falls, Montana." She flicked the card against her fingers, her expression thoughtful. "You think she'd pay that much for it, if I hauled it up to Montana myself?"

"Don't take a dime less," he advised.

The woman drew in a deep breath then slowly exhaled it. "Well, Mister, drinks are on the house. Come tomorrow, I'll be wrapping up my lady and going to Great Falls."

"Why I thought she was your girl, worked for you like girls in a bar used to do?"

"Mister, in ten years, she couldn't earn me that much from that bunch of old devils who come in here to drool

over her." She leaned her elbows on the bar with her back
to him and admired the painting. "Say, do you know the
artist? You seem to know a lot about all this."

"Who me?" he asked. When she turned and frowned
skeptically at him, he handed her the empty mug to refill.
"To be honest, I do know him. We drank a few beers
together. Squeezed a couple of gals like that one. He was
always drawing and painting for his bar bills. But let me
tell you, his young wife, Nancy really cleaned his nose.
Now she's selling his old paintings for big bucks. I thought
she'd bought every one of the buck naked ones in the
country. Guess she has, except for her." He motioned to the
picture.

"Well! Guess I never heard of this guy."

"Old Charlie was a good guy to ride with," Lacey said
with a grin as his recollection of past times filled his
thoughts.

"I'll get you another beer. That's the name on the skull
in the corner. Charlie Russell. Whew! Two thousand
dollars. Are you sure that she'll pay that much?" the
woman asked again.

"Yeah, she'll pay it," he said dryly. With a feeling of
loss tugging at his conscience, he studied the painting. It
would be a damned shame. Nancy Russell would sure as
the devil burn it as soon as she owned it. But hell,
everything else was gone. Charlie's last naked lady might
as well be too.

Between Jobs

Eagle feathers in their braids twisted in the wind. The white, yellow, and red greasy war paint on their hard-set faces and earth-red chests glistened in the sun. Small copper bells on their knee high boots faintly jingled as they rode single file though the scrub juniper trees; their small bare-foot horses softly crunched their way down the mountain side. Bows and rifles bristled in the warriors' rock-hard arms—their dark eyes seemed to scan everything in the canyon.

Rip quietly lowered himself behind the boulders. Relieved the Apaches had not seen him, he sprawled belly down and waited on their passing. The pitted barrel of the Colt .44 so close to his nose, he could smell the spend black powder's sharpness. He glanced at his weather beaten felt wide-brimmed hat on the ground beside him. His mouth formed a wry scowl of disgust over his tenuous situation. He had never expected to run into an Apache war party. The short cut he had chosen across the broken Verde River country might very well prove his undoing.

He dared take another peek. In disbelief, he blinked, taken aback at the sight of her golden hair and blue calico dress. A white woman captive rode a bald faced horse led by one of the bucks. A cry of protest rose in his throat as he watched her grip the horse's mane to stay seated. Then he thought of his own safety and silently dropped back down.

Damn, he wanted to look at her again but he hardly dared the risk. She was beautiful. His stomach rolled at the notion. Had he seen a mirage? Some sort of hallucination? While he crouched and listened to the soft drum of hooves, he became convinced he had actually seen a white female captive. What were those thieving no good redskins doing with her? He drew a deep breath for control for he could hardly contain himself at the prospect of her fate.

How could he save her? Someone's wife or daughter, surely there were folks out looking for her. But one man against ten Apache bucks—no-no, the odds were too great. Besides he was not an Injun fighter or scout—he was just an unemployed cowboy heading for work, he hoped. The new job near Prescott wouldn't be open for long—if he didn't get his gear and horse there shortly, some other cowpoke would have his place at the Quarter Circle T's bunkhouse.

The Apaches gone by, he rose to his feet studying where they had ridden down into the canyon. What would they do with the woman? The thought of her captivity only troubled him more as he headed for his picketed horse behind a screen of juniper. The bay gelding snatched a mouthful of sun-cured grass and twisted the blades into his mouth before raising his head at Rip's approach. At least Buck had not nickered at the Apache ponies.

"Buck," he said absently to the horse as he coiled up the lead rope. "We've got ourselves in a pickle barrel. Them Injuns have taken a white woman and we just can't let that go on. I saw her too. She's pretty as any—well, I thought she was." He tied the lariat on the saddle horn and gave a quick check in the direction the Apaches had disappeared. Nothing. He mounted, uncertain about his next move, he reined up the horse to stop for a minute and meditated on what he should do. The roiling in his intestines increased.

Only a damn fool would try to rescue that woman—but Rip Fisher had done stupider things in his lifetime. His mind set, he knew was going after her. The Winchester rifle under his stirrup fender was loaded to the gate with fresh ammo and he had an extra thirty rounds in his saddlebags for it and the Colt. More ammunition than he normally packed, but he'd bought the box of ammo to shoot game for his supper en route to his new job.

If he spent much time playing Injun fighter, he'd probably lose the position at the Quarter Circle T. Still, he knew as he booted Buck after them, that someone had to save her. Looked like he was elected. His impression of the blonde captive reminded him of a fine woman under a parasol he had once stepped aside for in Fort Worth. Her skin snow white, her eyes blue as the mountain skies and the dress's hoop seemed to flow as she held the skirt to save the rim bumping against him or Shorty Carr. Maybe it was her, the woman from Fort Worth who those Apache devils had kidnapped. Rip shook his head in dread.

Hours later, the sign of smoke in the cottonwood tops gave him his first clue he was nearing their camp. Apaches never made much fire, but he saw the faint traces and being forewarned he halted to hide Buck in a thicket under the rim rock. He wasn't certain of his actual location but the Apaches were camped along the Verde River. In the distance he could hear water's rush and children screaming as they played in the river. Dread filled, he swallowed around a great lump in his throat and drew a deep breath for strength. Before he found this woman and they were either killed or escaped, he would need to become a lot tougher. His weak legs barely supported him as he cautiously advanced on the Apaches. Sneaking up on a band of Apaches could be a tall order—these savages were experienced at warfare, and he was not.

He listened carefully as he worked his way slowly around the bushy junipers. The pungent-smelling evergreens offered him cover. His hands wet with sweat from grasping the rifle, he dried them one at a time on his jean legs and then resumed stalking forward.

Finally he viewed the camp. A few brush wickiups, some covered with yellow canvas, the squaws busy grinding corn or packing in bundles of firewood sticks. The children were splashing in the river and shouting in shrill voices. Their naked copper bodies gleamed under the mid day sun. The pony herd grazed across the river beyond the kids.

Where was the white woman? he studied the camp for a sign of her. Did some rutting buck have her inside? He felt nauseated standing behind the branches, the Winchester ready and she was nowhere in view.

Any moment they would probably discover him. Where was she? Then he saw the top of her golden hair as she came up the bank from the river bearing two canvas pails of water. Her shoulders slumped; he could not see her downcast face.

There was not a sign of a single warrior. Perhaps they were all sleeping. He wanted an extra horse for her to ride. Carrying double, Buck would never outrun them for long and they surely would pursue him if Rip took her away. But the Apaches horses were too far away for him to steal. His head pounded at the temples; there was too much for one man to think about. He wanted her out of that camp and he wanted the two of them to be gone.

Brash and bold sometimes worked. If he could manage to get the girl's attention before she ran off—he checked the rifle chamber. In the confusion, he needed to send the Apaches running in fear to the river and their horses. But Apaches weren't like Comanches back in Texas. Horses weren't their gods. Apaches ran on foot as fast as they did on horseback. But they had women and children here—even that was not a real concern like the plains tribes. He understood from newspaper reports that Apache women even smothered their newborns to save detection while retreating from the Army.

The white woman looked dejected with her head bowed standing among several squaws squatted and busy cooking. The time came for him to take action. He cocked the Winchester and took aim across the river at the pony herd. He wanted them to bolt at his shot and cause confusion with the Apaches for a moment on how many were attacking their camp.

The rifle's sharp roar drew plenty of black eyes. The bullet plowed up dust, the ponies broke and ran despite several youthful herders with switches trying to hold them. Squaws snatched up their babies and without looking ran screaming for the river.

"Wait! Stay there!" Rip shouted as he ran to get her. The enemy seemed routed for the moment.

A warrior exploded from a wickiup loading his single shot rifle. Rip drew a bead and fired. The hard hit Indian fell on the lodge and slumped to the ground. The black smoke cleared as he reached out to capture the woman's arm.

"Come with me," he shouted at her. He fired more rounds at the heels of the retreating squaws.

The woman looked at him without expression. Her long slender face was sunburned raw and pealing. He felt a pang of concern and sadness for her condition. Up close the dress was not nearly as fresh as he had envisioned it. Dirty and torn, the material looked very thin, only her yellow hair appeared well groomed.

"Come on," he repeated. "We haven't got time for much talk. I'm Rip Fisher and we need to vamoose."

"Vamoose?" she asked dully as if the word was foreign to her.

"Get out of here before they figure that I'm not the army."

"Oh."

Impatiently he pulled on her sleeve and watching their back trail, he lead her from the camp.

"We must tell Poco too" she muttered, stumbling as he tried to hurry her.

He wondered if there was another captive by that name she called out, but there was no time to check. They might not make another hundred yards before all hell broke loose.

"Lady, don't worry," he pleaded, anxious for her to keep up. "I am here to take you back home."

She never answered him. Still no sign of any threat. Where were the warriors who brought her in? Only one Indian with a gun? Would the Apaches close off their route of escape? He wished she would simply hurry. The trials of her captivity must have stopped her thinking clearly.

"Mount up, I'll ride behind you," he ordered when they reached his horse. he was beside himself over her dullness and lack of concern. He looked all around expecting any moment the blood thirsty faces of a dozen armed renegades to appear on the rim above them.

He swung up behind her, reached around her for the reins and booted Buck out of the brush and on the trail. The powerful Texas horse cat-hopped up the steep path with Rip unable to look back toward the camp, but fully expecting to hear the war cries closing in.

Late afternoon and sundown closed the curtain on their day with no sign of pursuit. He finally reined Buck to a halt on top of the high range, where he could survey much of the country they'd crossed since their escape.

"I want to see if they're after us," he said. He dismounted and scanned the mountainside beneath them. Nothing, but that was no sign the Apaches weren't on their back trail. She had never answered him.

He looked back at her. She sat woodenly on the horse. Her hands clutched the saddle horn. Her blue eyes just stared at some point in the darkening eastern sky.

"What's your name?" he asked, helping her down.

She looked around as if she was more concerned with her body functions than answering him.

"I'll turn my back," he said and took Buck's reins to lead him away a few yards.

"Don't go," she said.

Rip nodded he understood she did not want him to leave her. He halted with his back to her feeling like an intruder in her life as he waited.

"The Apaches won't bother us before sunup," he said to fill in the silence between them. "They're superstitious about night. Something about being taken to Hell if they get killed in the darkness."

No answer. He wondered if she was still back there. Had the Apaches destroyed her mind? He remembered a white girl of fourteen who the Army brought into Fort Concho. She had a doll she held like a baby and rocked it all the time. Never talked to anyone but the doll. Soldiers said her part Injun baby had died and the doll was its substitute. The Comanche captivity had vexed her mind.

"Are you hungry?" he asked and waited.

No answer.

Then he felt her slender fingers close on his arm and she stood beside him. He glanced at her for a second. She was trembling even the hand hold on his arm was shaky. Her eyes stared past him at the layers of mountain ranges.

"Clyde, we must go home," she said and then drew her shoulders back in resolve.

"I'm not—" Then he cut off his denial to her. Clyde must have been her husband. "Do you know the way?" he asked hoping she could tell him something."

"Bloody Basin, of course."

"Sure," Rip said and tried to hid his disappointment. She wasn't in her right mind.

The sliver of a moon made enough light for them to travel by. Rip headed southwest toward the Bloody Basin country. Perhaps she would lead herself home. He hoped so.

Several times during the night he caught her by the waist when she dropped asleep and nearly pitched face first off the horse. Each time after he had set her up in the saddle, he felt a twinge of guilt being so familiar with a woman he did not even know by name. Each time she passed out, he offered to stop and let her rest, but she shook her head, no.

Dawn came with her pointing a limp arm in a vague direction; they followed a wagon track road most of the day. She seemed to be familiar with the country and he hoped they would soon find her people. Someone would be very glad to have their wife-mother what-ever back, he felt certain. As the day wore on, Buck began stumbling a lot and showing his tiredness.

"Home," she said and pointed toward a grove of cottonwoods in the draw.

Rip drew a deep breath in relief. He slipped off Buck and took the reins to lead the horse the rest of the way. He didn't want her people to think he'd taken any liberties with a woman in her mind set. It hurt him to even look at her. Would she ever be normal again? But her condition wasn't his problem, he'd done enough shooting up that Apache camp and taking her away from them—he still felt good about her rescue.

The top knotted quail whistled their sharp notes around them and the wind fresh with the juniper-pinyon smell filled Rip's nose. His boot heels teetered around in the loose rocks going downhill; he could see the corrals and some adobe buildings. Elated, he practically had her home, he wondered if she had any children.

Strange no dog barked, most folks kept several around their headquarters because they helped keep the Indians away. He rounded a large juniper and found the corral gates open and empty. Disappointed and struck with the truth, he observed the abandoned adobe house without a front door. Then he saw the three crosses on the mounds—graves. They weren't fresh either maybe a month or so old. How long had the Apaches held her? God only knew.

"They're dead aren't they?" she asked.

He turned quickly at her even words. "Yes ma'am." He studied her for a long time. What would she do next? When she started to dismount, he helped her down.

She wrung her hands so hard, he hurt for her. Unmoved she remained standing in place as if afraid to check on anything more.

"I had to tell myself all the time I was captive that they were alive," she began, trying to hold in her sorrow. "You knew they killed my baby son Travis that first day they kidnapped me?" She held her hand up to stay him from helping her. "I'm fine, Mister Fisher. That is your name?"

"Yes." Rip was taken back by her words. Had she known all along he wasn't her man or had she just begun to realize their identities? Rip felt relieved she knew that much for the moment.

"Clyde my husband, my seven year old daughter Bonnie and a Mexican boy Poco who worked for my husband must be buried there." She motioned to the graves. "Every day I kept telling myself that they were still alive. You know that was how I survived?"

"Yes ma'am." He saw the tears well up in her eyes.

Uncomfortable and feeling inadequate, he glanced around. She had no one left. This ranch sure needed a lot of fixing. Clyde must have had some branded cattle on the range. She caught Rip by the sleeve and buried her face in his chest. The wetness quickly soaked through his vest and shirt. His arms gingerly comforted her. There would always be another job.

"You won't just leave me will you?"

He finally grasped her by the shoulders and looked down into her tear swamped eyes. "No, I won't leave you, but please tell me your name."

"Dallas." She blinked her thick wet lashes and for the first time he saw life in her blue eyes as she looked back at him. He gently folded her against his chest. Dallas wasn't a far piece from Fort Worth. He'd finally found his own version of the woman with the hoop skirt.

Road to Baghdad

Salome studied the garish mural on the peddler's van. The artist had depicted her in a belly dancing costume. The pillowing silk pants, the gauzy veils and her bare stomach that always drew stares. In the picture, her breasts were larger and her legs longer than in reality. Still the painting mirrored her bobbed black wig and heavily made up face.

Jo Jo's scream brought her thoughts back to the present. She frowned at the excited monkey, then smiled in sympathy at him. The pitiful little beggar, who collected coins in a cup during her performances, was chained in the shade beneath the wagon.

Sidney Foster, her manager-promoter, had taken the busted wagon wheel to the next settlement to be repaired. He left her alone in the oven hot desert. Somewhere west lay civilization, in the form of the next stop, the mining camp of Baghdad. According to Sidney, Baghdad was flush with gold. Around her was only the monotonous sea of brownish gray brush, studded with hovering, armed cactus and distant islands of purple mountains. The one sign of humanity was the road made up of two dusty ruts that ran from whence they came to where they must go.

Salome did not miss Sidney's company. She considered him obnoxious with his paunchy stomach and his bald dome which he kept hidden under a bowler hat.

Before Sidney left, he had spoken harshly to her. "Watch out for yourself. Mind me, girl!"

The arrogant barker protected her virtue like a jailer, but only out of fear that if she became large with child, his golden goose might waddle instead of swaying provocatively. Since joining him, she had danced atop bars

139

in saloons, on stages with real painted scenery backdrops, even in wagon beds on the trail west from St Louis to this God forsaken waste land where they had broken down.

In the Arizona Territory with its endless desert, they traveled from gold camp to gold camp, but despite the large crowds she drew, she and Sidney were always broke. She knew the reason for their poverty. Sidney could not resist cards, whiskey or loose women. Reeking of cheap perfume and sour whiskey, late at night he would crawl back to sleep in his own bunk opposite hers. Salome feigned sleep on those nights, lest he lay a sweaty palm on her. The memory of his repulsive touch disgusted her; she shivered in the desert heat. Because of the soaring temperatures, all she wore was a thin shift. She sighed and looked toward the distant mountains. Nothing had changed; Sidney would blow whatever money he had in his pocket before he returned.

They had moved from one boomtown site to the next. She recalled his barking pitch, enticing men to see the dance of Eve.

"You can be Adam again with the first woman on earth," Sidney would promise them. In her first act, she danced with a large serpent called Mohammed. The snake was depicted on the side of the wagon in proportions far beyond its actual size. After Eve's snake dance, there would be an intermission while Sidney collected more money, because by then the men wanted to see even more of her. Her second dance was patterned after her namesake, Salome. It was the same dance that cost the saint, John the Baptist, his life.

Jo Jo would bounce around while she performed, his tin cup outstretched, clinking to the tune of double eagles and even gold nuggets. Generosity was a weakness with her audiences and Sidney capitalized on it. He was, after all, well versed at losing his own money. In Tombstone they had been so successful, Salome had been certain not even a wastrel like Sidney could spend so much wealth. However, the master squanderer had found faro and poker too great a temptation.

Whenever at last a new attraction came to town and enticed the drooling customers away, the two of them packed up for more fertile ground.

Salome, her innocent dreams of riches slowly dying, realized there would never be enough profit to divide. She schemed for a way to save a small portion for herself from each performance. However, Sidney kept the purse strings pulled tight; she only observed him counting the take. There had to be a way for her to get her fair share. Salome shook her head as she watched Jo Jo eating the crust of bread that she had given him.

"You poor monkey tethered on your chain, we're alike," she said softly. His restrains were like her own. She too was leashed to the van by invisible bonds.

Mohammed, the six-foot boa constrictor, was content in his wicker hamper. The desert's searing heat suited him. Later she would offer him a drink. He usually slept undisturbed until it was time for him to perform. Then she would command him to do her bidding, just as she dance to the master puppeteer's wishes.

Salome cocked her head and listened intently. Someone was singing out in the desert. The shift wrapped tightly around her, she wondered if she was hearing things. No, she decided, she was not imaging the sound. Someone was coming and it definitely was not the stagecoach, for the one going east was not due to pass until sundown.

A man's voice carried across the greasewood. When he appeared, leading a sleepy eyed burro, Salome could see that beneath the man's floppy hat, he was gray whiskered.

"Whoa!" The man came to an abrupt halt. He blinked his eyes and shook his head. "Girl, are you a mirage?"

Salome hid a smile. "No," she said softly. This desert vagrant did not appear dangerous, but she backed toward the protection of the wagon, watching him doff his hat and stare wide-eyed at the mural.

"If that picture is truly you, then perhaps I'm in heaven?"

Amused at his bewilderment, she responded in jest. "It's too hot for heaven."

He chuckled. "Yeah, you're right about that. Them preachers were wrong. Nobody would give up their sinning ways if they knowed this was hell and you'd be here." His cackling laughter echoed in the desert.

"My name is Salome," she introduced herself. "What's yours?"

"Harold." He paused and shook his head. "Girl, years ago I read all about you in the bible. You danced for Herod till he promised you John the Baptist's head. I know about the serpent and Eve too. I know why you're here and why I'm here too."

Salome had no idea what the old man was rambling about, but she considered it safe to let him talk. She folded her arms in front of her and tried to look interested.

"Dad rat, it's my luck again," the man growled in disgust. "Me finding the mother lode and the devil's come to get me. Pardon me, ma'am, but I never expected him to send his handmaiden."

Salome blinked, started to open her mouth to set the man straight, but instead she shut it. A wave of pity for him washed over her. Let him think what he wanted of her. She watched as he turned and removed a canvas bag from his pack.

"Myra," he spoke with his burro, "I've got us in a mess and I'm sorry about that, girl. But, there maybe a way for us to get out." Salome could barely make out his next words. "...going to buy our way out of hell."

What did he mean? Her pulse quickened, this desert drifter must be near mad from his solitary existence. Before she could conjure up the words to gently dissuade him, her glance became galvanized by the gold granules that he poured into his palm.

"Now see here what I've got, but then you already knowed I had it, didn't you, Salome?"

Shaken by the vision of his riches, she stepped closer to examine the glittering dust in his hand.

"That's the reason you're here," he accused her. "I know ever time I strike it rich, I've always craved flesh and cards. But why tell you? You know how I've wasted it time and again. No matter I want to see that dance you did for Herod. And that snake on the sign, he's here too, ain't he?"

"Yes." She felt sad for the man. He acted so confused, she worried about him. He was much older than she had first thought and his brown eyes held a pleading note that she could not ignore. She was not frightened by this prospector and she certainly did not mind performing for him. In other places she had danced for much worse than the likes of him, usually for very little gain, thanks to Sidney. Besides, if Harold insisted that she take a few granules of gold in exchange for entertaining him, she would be that much closer to getting away from her keeper.

"Mohammed is here, too," she finally said. "Do you want to see both dances?"

"Yes, yes. I'll pay you for both of them, but then you got to promise to let us go. Both Myra and me. Do you promise, Salome?"

She lowered her face to hide a smile. He obviously considered her some type of siren or a witch. But she could hardly blame the poor man. Who would have expected to come upon someone like her in such a barren wasteland?

"I will do that. It will take a little time for me to prepare," she warned him. She would need a stage of some kind. Glancing around, she noticed the gray rock wall in the dry wash beside the road.

"Have we got a deal?" he persisted.

Clasping her hands in front of her, she bowed slightly. "Yes, we have a deal" Then she pointed to the gully. "You must go to the dry wash over there and wait."

"Dag nab it, Myra, we've struck a deal!"

"Wait!" she ordered. This new role for her was beginning to be fun and she knew intuitively that this man expected a commanding tone from her. "Take that canvas chair down there and place it on the edge of the sand bar for you to sit on."

"Yes sirree. What else?" he asked excited. "What else you want me to do?"

She straightened her shoulders, fully prepared to give the old man something to remember for the rest of his lonely life. "When you hear my words, close your eyes. Do you understand?"

"Oh, yes. I will. I'll do just as you say."

"Go now and wait in your chair."

"Yes ma'am. I'll take Myra too, cause she's putting up her half."

Afraid she would burst out laughing, she turned and hurried inside the van. She closed the dusty curtain over the rear of the wagon so he could not see inside, should he decide to peek. Her fingers trembled unaccountably as she fumbled with the sash on her shift. Quickly she stepped out of the filmy garment and stood naked in the close confine of the wagon. The air was hot and stifling, bringing out fresh beads of perspiration on her olive skin.

Confidently, she began her ritual. She poured fine scented oil in her palms and began to rub it into her skin. Soon her legs were glistening in the shadowy light. Then her supple belly, firm breasts, arms and face received a ritualistic coating of oil.

Carefully she shadowed her eyes with black grease paint. If the old man gave her a few gold granules, it might be enough for her to escape Sidney's bondage. She tried to suppress her own excitement, not wanting her hopes to become too high, but she found it an effort to ignore her apparent good luck.

She prepared the wig careful to hide her own Dutch boy bob. Her hands shaking with anticipation, Salome vowed she would dance for this prospector as she had never danced before.

Not even the hated black hairpiece that resembled Cleopatra's would dampen her spirits this time. After slipping large gold hoops through her ears, she drew out the gold chains from her wooden jewelry box. Sidney had told her they were real, but she doubted him. Wetting her lips, she looked in the mirror and spoke aloud, "You can be Salome or plain old Nelda Greenbaum whenever you get away from Sidney."

The baggy silk pants slid on easily and she stood to tie them at the waist. Next, she draped the gauzy veils in place. She was ready. The smoky mirror revealed to her the girl outside on the painting. All she needed to complete the picture were her Arabic prayer rug and her dance partner Mohammed.

With the carpet under one arm, she picked up the serpent's hamper and climbed out of the van. As she crossed to the makeshift stage, she noticed that Harold was seated below, his face turned away.

"Close your eyes," she commanded in a loud voice.

"Promise to . . . I ain't looking."

She looked down. His hands gripped the armrests, she felt certain his eyes matched them. Salome smiled at her new found power and hurried to her stage.

A platform of diamond sparkling sand shone under the sun's highest zenith. Mohammed's basket was in place and the prayer rug rolled out. Salome stood back to face her audience.

Her arms folded over the layers, she spoke, "Harold, open your eyes."

He seemed to brace himself in the chair as his eyelids fluttered.

"Oh, my Gawd—I'm sorry. It's just I couldn't believe that painting and that there really was someone like you."

Salome noted three canvas bags at his feet. Hastily, she drew her eyes away from the tempting sight.

"You must stay in your chair," she warned him, "until the dance is over." When he did not answer her, a knot formed in her throat as she worried what he expected from her. She gambled. "Do you have payment?"

"Yes, ma'am. Right here." He pointed to the pouches at his feet. "I promise you I'll be on my best behavior."

"Very good," she said, controlling her breathing. "The dance will begin."

Salome knelt before the basket and wound her arm in with the serpent. She had no doubts that Mohammed would begin his circling journey to her neck as cued. The snake responded. When she stepped back and began to dance, he slowly began to encircle her. The scales sliding under his powerful muscles rubbed her nipples hard in passing over her breasts. The turgid coils girdled her waist with the firmness of a lover's hands.

Mohammed's angular head darted about, watching, as though he was her guardian. Slowly his body threaded between her legs and emerged around her right thigh. The ribbed structure brushed her in private pleasure. As he continued his sensuous journey down her body, her belly was free to rise and fall with the gentle gyrations of her hips. Then as if ordered, the serpent began his slow ascent up her body. His retreat quickened her breathing and in response, her dance became more demanding. Salome began to hear the bawdy shouts and lurid jeers of hundreds of men. Though always ghostly and far away, she could still hear them. The sounds did not diminish the pleasure she experienced whenever she performed.

When she knelt to put the serpent back, she noticed Harold's pallor.

"You've seen the first dance," she said softly, realizing Sidney was not there as usual to collect the money.

He tossed something that struck heavy in the sand. Her breath caught in her throat. Swallowing back her excitement least she destroy his image of her, she rose and began to hum. The sun glinted on her jewelry. Then she looked directly into Harold's eyes.

She saw that the cob-webbed recesses of his brain had been cleared. The youthful clarity of Adam replaced his former look. Yes, she had transformed Harold into becoming the first man, Adam. The serpent had shown him, lied, promised, coerced him into believing this was Eden and she was the first Eve. The power of Harold's manhood had been restored at this dry fountain of youth. Salome knew Harold could taste the apple. One at a time, she shed the layers of gauzy veils which fluttered to the sparkling stage floor. Her body became a loom. Dreamlike, she wove a promise for her audience that grew in intensity with each discarded thread.

Salome knew her power. Men would scream for her to go faster, as though she could deliver some relief from the pressures building within their skulls. They wanted her to help them escape the obsession that she had created.

Then the dance was over.

She dropped to the prayer rug and knelt; the last vestige of strength drained from her body.

The thud of two more heavy objects struck the sand. The sound took her breath. Deliberate, she kept her eyes closed, afraid to open them and discover that she had merely dreamed the entire episode.

"Yes, sirree." Harold's voice sounded dry and weak. "I've spent fortunes on a lot less than your dancing. I'm obliged for mine and Myra's freedom. We'll be going, before you change your mind about releasing us."

Salome raised up. She studied the man's back, his step lighter; his shoulders thrown back like a younger man. She could faintly hear his prattle with the burro.

"Yes, Myra, you seen things that ain't been done on this earth in thousands of years. Best of all, we've escaped old Lucifer again... but it's mighty sure he's around here somewhere."

Salome expected him to look back, but he did not. With weak hands, she reached for the nearest canvas bag. Her heart raced and her ragged pulse beat at her throat as she fumbled with the drawstrings.

Gold dust. Each bag was full to the seams with genuine gold. A fortune was hers. Tears blinded her as she considered what she must do next.

Burdened by the heavy gold pouches that she hugged in her arms, Salome hurried to the van. The eastbound stage would soon be coming. Sidney could have the costume; she tore off the last veils. He could have the hated wig too, Salome threw it aside.

She viciously brushed her own hair and studied the image in the mirror to be sure she was not dreaming. The animals, Jo Jo and Mohammed must go along with her on the stagecoach. She could not leave them for Sidney to abuse. She had danced her last dance and played her last role as an enticer of men's dreams. And she'd given new life to one old man and his burro.

Wash Day

Her elbows dripping with sudsy water, Rhettia hoisted a pair of heavy sodden pants from the tub. The muscles between her slender shoulder blades complained as she tossed the soapy britches into the rinse tub.

Hands on her hips, she arched her back to ease the dull ache at the base. The thin blouse that hugged her breasts was soaked down the front and the material strained against her nipples. She pushed back her wavy brown hair, then bent to remove another pair of pants.

Horse hooves clumped on the hard ground in the alley. Rhettia paused. One rider—perhaps more—were coming up past her tall backyard fence. When they passed the place where the board was missing, she craned her head to see who it was.

An iron gray horse entered her vision, the rider wearing a canvas duster. Her eyes widened as the man dismounted and opened the gate.

"Ma'am," he said in a very cultured sounding drawl. "I'm sorry to interrupt, but I need to check my horse's shoe. Do you mind?"

Too shocked to speak, she shook her head woodenly. He turned his back to her and raised the gray horse's foot.

She was curious about him, guessing his age to be mid-thirties. He was slender, under six foot tall. Because of the duster, she couldn't see if he wore a side arm but the brass plate of a rifle glistened behind his stirrup.

He seemed to hold the hoof up for a long time. Rhettia dried her hands on a rag as she waited for him to release it and straighten up. When she glanced down, she blinked in horror at the dark rings of her nipples and she quickly turned her back to him. Her face grew hot with embarrassment. What should she do to cover herself?

"Ma'am?" the stranger asked quietly. "Could you spare me a tall drink of water?"

She started to turn then noticed the shawl on the short line across the porch. She pulled it free by the corner and covered her shoulders, draping the ends over her breasts to conceal her exposure.

"Yes," she said. "I'll get one from the house."

He thanked her and turned back to check his saddle. As she went indoors for his water, Rhettia wondered what the stranger did for a living.

When she returned, he stood at the edge of the porch stoop. His good looks shocked her. He was very tanned with a strong lean face. She offered him a demure nod as she handed him the glass.

"I certainly appreciate this. I'm sorry I've interrupted your work."

She watched him take a long swallow, his Adam's apple moving smoothly.

"I needed a break anyway."

"Yes, washing clothes is hard work." He looked around the small yard. "I've never lived in town. Guess I never realized how crowded it was."

Rhettia wondered where he lived.

"Thanks," he returned the glass and dug in his shirt pocket, producing a silver dollar that he held out for her to take.

Shocked at the idea of someone paying a dollar for a drink of water, she quickly refused his generosity. The stranger closed his hand over the dollar and walked away.

Rhettia watched him gather his reins and slip them over the gray horse's head. But he turned back before she could avert her eyes and his warm smile caused her to blush. He reined the horse around, then with a devilish laugh, he flipped the coin into her washtub.

He looked right at her. "Jesse James always pays his debts." Then like a gentleman touched the wide brim of his hat. "Have a good day, ma'am."

Jesse James? Rhettia's breath caught in her throat. Numb, she watched him hold the gate open and nudge the horse with his heel into the alley.

What was Jesse James doing in Minnesota? Should she warn the authorities? But he seemed so polite? All those stories about Jesse being a killer and outlaw, why this man must not have been the same one. With a shake of her head, she went back to her tubs. Reaching down in the water, she seined out the dollar from among the sunken clothes.

Down the street, gunfire abruptly disrupted the quiet afternoon. Rhettia's head jerked up as she listened to the distant shooting.

Well, maybe the stories had been true after all. With a shrug, she put the dollar in her skirt pocket and bent back over the washtub.

Bitter Wind

The blue sky was all he could see. Cold seeped into Jake's clothing. Lying on his back was why all he saw was the damn sky. If he turned, his cheek would be in the snow. Warm blood leaked out of the bullet hole in his side, soaked through his shirt into the fleece-lined jacket and puddled under his back.

Too weak to rise, now, how much precious blood would he spill before he died? Fighting to remain conscious, he wondered if angels would come for him. Jake had seen such winged messengers. They were naked, painted on a canvas in the Silver Dollar Saloon. In his final hours on earth he'd like to see naked angels. Maybe they'd even hug him and make him warm again.

Damn, he'd soon die out in the middle of no-where, ten miles west of Dodge. Jake Mahaffey would expire. His whole body shivered, just awful cold dying.

No angels without clothes were coming for him. Who was he trying to fool? Not himself, certainly not some God he didn't believe in, not in these last moments of his life, there would be no heavenly intervention for Jake Mahaffey.

He needed a drink of whiskey. Liquor with a kick. Real fire water that would burn his throat going down; even heat his ears. Why didn't some barkeep come by? He had money to pay him—lots of money.

Jake thought of Thelma. Her voluptuous body spilling out of her satin undergarments standing before him. Two pillows for lips, the curve of her sensuous belly, the pleasure between her short legs. The notion warmed him more than the dead January sun overhead. If Thelma knew of his condition, she would cry and beg him not to die. He hoped she'd cry later, when she learned the news of his death. No one else would.

Jake could barely remember his mother, a breed who sold her body to enlisted soldiers. The lowest form of a dove, she died of TB at a very young age. Her death left Jake on his own as a pre-teen.

Vividly, Jake recalled the first man he'd ever shot. Silvan Cates, a broad shouldered bully with a matted beard, the breath of a gut eating dog and wearing dirt glazed buckskins. For no reason other than pure meanness, Silvan had knocked the thirteen-year-old Jake to the ground, then kicked him, spat on him and called him the spawn of scum.

It required two hours that day for Jake to steal a pistol. A cap and ball model, the Walker Colt was so heavy it took both of his hands to steady the muzzle. Jake strode into the sutler's store. To keep the Colt concealed, he cocked the hammer back by his side. Quickly before the shock of recognition could warn Cates, Jake raised the revolver and aimed at the man's heart. The shot blew Silvan Cates over backwards in his chair. There was a cloud of eye burning smoke and confusion in the room. Jake ran outside, stole Cates' horse and fled Fort Laramie. From then on Jake lived by the gun and his wits.

He preyed on the defenseless. The single traveler or an individual wagon on the trail became his victims. Jake robbed, raped, and murdered and he let the Indians have the blame.

When his eyelids grew heavy, Jake shut them. At last he began to feel warm. Earlier that morning, he had trailed the Texan out of Dodge. Flush with cattle sales money, the soft spoken rancher looked like an easy target. Jake expected to enjoy a lush time all winter on the proceeds from this robbery and murder.

But as life's final ebb tide began to drain away, Jake managed to ask one last question aloud. "How in hell's name could such a slow talker have been so damn fast with a gun?"

The bitter wind answered him, but only Jake heard, then he died.

California Jones

Cal blinked his burning eyes, wondering if the haze of his hangover was distorting his vision. A woman stood at the foot of his bed and she definitely was not the usual sort of female that frequented his shack in Tucson's shanty row. This particular gal wore a spotless starched dress She was a lady and he didn't have the faintest notion what she was doing in his place.

"California Jones?" she asked in a very cultured voice.

Cal sat up straight on the bed and scowled in pained disbelief at her beauty.

"I might be Jones," he said with that he scratched his left ear and then tossed aside the thin green blanket, exposing his faded red underwear.

The woman gasped and quickly turned her face away.

"That's right, you look off over there and I'll get dressed."

"You are California Jones?" she asked, sounding concerned about his true identity.

Who in the cat hair did she think he was? Wyatt Earp? He nodded in admission as he pulled on his waist overalls, then he realized she was not looking at him and spoke up in a gruff voice. "That's my name. What's yours lady?"

"Colleen Swain."

He wrinkled his nose at the sour smelling shirt he picked off the nail on the wall. Never heard of her before. He frowned and silently repeated her name to himself as if to draw recognition from some recesses of his foggy brain. It still meant nothing to him.

"Don't reckon we've ever met," he said as he shoved his arms into the shirt. "You can turn around now," he said, primed for her next move. "If you come to preach for my soul, save your breath, sister. Better men than you have tried before. I don't give to needy causes either because I ain't got nothing and besides I like my way of life and ain't fixing to change."

She raised her chin up, drew her shoulders back. "I have come here on business."

"What kinda business?" he asked, taken back.

"I've come to hire you."

"I don't take care of no lawns and gardens. Go two doors down. That old Messikin, Jesus Juarez, he'll help you." He pointed in that direction. but she stood unwavering and he began to wonder what her real purpose was in being there.

"The Apaches have taken my son. I want him back." She finished and chewed on her lower lip. Close to tears, she wrung her hands to control herself as she waited for his reply.

He shook his head slowly. "If the Apaches got your boy, you need the law or the army, ma'am. not me"

"But they've searched or so they tell me." Her blue eyes began to flood. She turned away and dappled at them with a small handkerchief. "My Teddy is out there, Mr. Jones and they haven't found a sign of him." She drew up her shoulders and turned to face him. "They say you can do things with the renegades."

He felt her stare. There was a time that he could have helped—he wanted to tell her something. Sunshine streamed in the dirt streaked windows illuminating her fine features. She looked to him like a gold nugget in a pile of debris. He dropped his head in defeat. "You've come to the wrong place for that kinda help."

He squeezed his eyes to shut out the pounding at his temples. His tongue felt too thick for his mouth—he needed a drink. Why didn't she leave—he'd done told her he couldn't help her. She wanted to pin him down. He avoided looking at her as the cot protested his sitting down on it.

"Go see the military." He stared at the floor for strength to tell her. "Look at me lady. I'm nothing like the man you want." His coughing began and it grew deeper until he bent over, fearing he would not stop until all his air was gone.

He waved her help away. Finally half strangled but regaining his breath, he looked up at the knock on the door. Who else was coming?

Before he could rise to answer it, Gladys Newton, his neighbor and drinking partner burst in. Gladys stopped at the sight of Mrs. Swain and clasped her hand to her mouth.

"Hell, Cal. Why excuse me?" Her paunchy figure blocked the doorway, she acted undecided whether to come in or not. She drew in a deep breath exposing a generous portion of her large bosom in the low cut dress. "I didn't realize you had company."

"This here's Mrs. Swain. But she's leaving," he said with a wave of his hand. "But you could have saved yourself a trip. Ain't a drop of anything to drink left in this house."

With some effort, Gladys came inside and looked at the stranger. "Nice to meetcha ma'am." At that point, she kind of curtsied as much as her fat legs would bend. "Any friend of Cal's is a friend of mine."

"Yes, er—nice to meet you too, Gladys."

"By gad, Jonesy," Gladys said with a knowing chuckle and a wink at him, "You got yourself a real looker this time. I better get back—over there. And let you two get on with—ah, your business, huh?"

"Go on Gladys," he said in disapproval as she lumbered out the door laughing like a hyena. "Don't mind her, ma'am, she don't mean no harm."

"I guess you can see, I'm not easily put off Mr. Jones," Colleen said, with a deep swallow to punctuate her sentence. "I want you to bring my son back to me."

Cal sighed aloud. Why did this stubborn woman persist to torment him? "Lady, if them Apaches did take him and I'm saying that because you need to know, he more than likely is dead by now—"

She gave him a short nod to continue. She was tough, he decided, but she better realize the chances that boy was dead were ten times more likely than finding him alive.

"Why I don't even have a horse or anything."

She pounced like a mountain lion on his excuse. "You can use my late husband's things. I'll get you any supplies you need."

Cal knew he was licked. She would never leave until she'd badgered him into going on this wild goose chase. "I should have figured you was a widow woman coming here all alone and all."

"Yes," she said subdued. "My husband was killed when they took Teddy captive."

Cal recalled something about the businessman getting murdered down on the San Pedro and the son being taken off by the raiders. He scratched the thin hair on top his head, trying to recall how long ago he'd heard of the raid.

"They say you know these people. That you once lived with them."

He nodded. "Some—I scouted and rode with them, but it was a long time ago."

"You're my last hope." She wet her lips and drew her shoulders back. "And if he—Teddy, is not alive then I want to I know that too." Then she shook her head so slightly. "It is the *not knowing* that is so hard."

He couldn't stand to watch her any longer; he dropped his gaze to the floor. What could it hurt? Besides he was flat broke and she would pay him to go search. He knew some camps in the mountains. But they were many miles from Tucson—could he even ride that far? What the hell? When he got back, he and Gladys would drink her money up and rejoice.

"Where's your place?" he asked.

"Then you'll take the job?"

"Hold on here." He held up both hands to settle her down. "I'll ride out in the hills and ask some Injuns I know. They may or may not have heard of this boy. He may be in old Mexico by now." He wanted to be certain she understood he might come back empty handed.

"I understand, Mr. Jones. I just know you will find Teddy."

"Where do you live?" he asked, feeling uncomfortable at her words.

"Oh yes, on Fifth Street, third house from the corner of Congress."

"I'll find you. Give me a quarter."

Colleen frowned at his outstretched hand. "What ever for?"

"I need a bath and a haircut, lady. I smell too bad to stay sober for long."

Without hesitation, she withdrew two quarter from her reticule and placed them in his hand.

"Thanks," he said and closed his fist over the coins. "I'll be along in an hour or so. Have someone saddle that horse, put some grub in a sack, couple small sacks of corn too and fill a couple of canteens with water." He scratched his right ear, something inside it was itching like hell. "I'll need a rifle and some shells." He rose and walked her to the door still deeply engrossed in his needs.

"I'll have it all ready. Will you need money to trade for him?"

"Money? No. Let's see, I'll need four or five bottle of whiskey. That should do it." He looked directly into her eyes, expecting to hear a protest at his demand for liquor. To his surprise, she quickly withdrew some bills from her purse and handed them to him.

"You'll have to buy it," she apologized and then she started for the rig parked at his fallen down yard gate.

"Ma'am," he called out to her. "Try not to worry yourself sick. If he's alive and in the country, mind you, I'll try to find him. Worrying won't help a thing."

She turned back dabbing at her eyes and forced a nod in gratitude. "Thank you, Mr. Jones."

Θ Θ Θ

Two hours later smelling like a Chinese laundry in his clean clothes and bathed, he arrived at her front door. He had allowed himself two short beers, which entitled him to a free boiled egg lunch at McCarthy's Saloon. On her front step, he belched loud enough to wake the dead, then rapped on her door. In the time between their meeting and his recovery, he had grown more doubtful about the boy's chances of being alive, but decided not to go over that with her again. She knew the risks—he certainly wasn't God.

"Oh, Mr. Jones, you've kept your word." She stepped back to invite him in.

"You figure I'd light out on some drunk?" he demanded.

"There were folks said,—"

"Listen, I been keeping my word all my life. That's beside the point, is that horse saddled?" He followed her into the spacious living room.

"Yes, he's ready out back."

"I hope we can wrap this whiskey better, so it makes the ride," he said showing her the poke he carried.

"I have some towels?"

"Sounds awfully good to use for that." He looked around her fine house and felt helpless at what else to wrap the glass bottles with.

"No, they would work." She rushed off to get some. A maid returned with her and they made quick work of wrapping the half dozen bottles of golden liquor. He didn't want to even look at the whiskey as they tied the Turkish towels with string at the neck of each quart. Damn he needed a drink—powerfully bad. His molars nearly floated away thinking how good the rye would taste flowing down his throat. He used his index finger to pry some breathing room between his neck and the stiff collar.

"There, Mr. Jones, they should ride that way," she said proudly as she repacked them in the cotton sack he intended to hang from the saddle horn.

He took the bag and then looked hard at the tile floor. "I don't want you to get your hopes all up. I may not find a thing out there."

Colleen shook her head violently. "I will not give up hope. My son is alive out there. I know it!"

"All right, Mrs. Swain." He followed her through the house, not satisfied that her intuition was right.

He rode out of Tucson on the powerful sorrel horse; the whiskey bottles in the tow sack against his left knee, the 44/40 under his right leg in the scabbard. In his shirt pocket he carried a tintype, the one she'd given him. Teddy looked like a strapping boy. Somewhere out there someone knew something about the lad's whereabouts or his demise. Cal's half squinted eyes studied through the glare of the desert, past the saw tooth mountains he would find the answer about Teddy's fate if he was lucky. His tongue grew thicker with each mile he rode, water never quenched the greater thirst.

Four days later, he still rode through the empty canyons. No wickiups, only a few old fire rings in the cactus forested hills where he had expected to locate some of them; he found no inhabited rancherias.

In late afternoon he crossed over a range and descended a narrow trail into a chasm. A hint of something teased his nose. When he drew closer, he spotted a grass wickiup under a palo verde. At last, he'd found a camp and the notion gave him new strength.

A bare-headed Apache male came out with a single shot rifle. Cal reined in his horse, his movement slow and non-hostile. He took a hard look at the man and surmised him to be a reservation deserter. The absence of black war paint was one clue; the other fact that convinced Cal was that the rifle was not cocked.

"You have come a long ways?" the Apache asked in his own tongue.

"Yes, but I am not the Army or the Indian police."

The man nodded he heard and waved for him to approach. "We once rode together. I know you."

Cal squinted to recall the man's name. A teenage girl came outside and took the reins to his horse.

"My woman will care for it," the Apache said regarding his horse. "My name is Billy Good and I remember yours, it is Jones."

Cal nodded he'd heard the man as he took a small sack from his saddlebags to give to her, before he let her have the reins. When she led the sorrel away he stepped closer to Billy.

"It's been a long time. Why aren't you at San Carlos?"

Billy never answered as he indicated to Cal to enter the lodge. He knew when Indians did not wish to speak of something, they ignored the question.

"I gave corn to your wife," he said. His host nodded in gratitude and motioned for him to be seated. Both men took seats on the frayed Navajo blanket spread on the ground. There was no food in sight.

She ducked in with the pouch of flat corn. Without any reaction, she poured it onto her grinding stone and began to crush it as the two men made small talk about old times.

"I came here on a mission," Cal finally said.

Billy nodded. He understood such things.

"Some broncos took a boy in a raid. A white boy—" He fished out Teddy's picture.

Billy studied the picture and then he showed it to the woman who nodded, she had seen it too. No clue, Cal knew he was playing poker with tough players—not an eyebrow twitched, not a mouth broke a straight line.

"His mother—she wants her son back. I have come to find him."

"What could you trade for such a boy?" Billy finally asked.

"Whiskey."

Billy nodded his head, "What else?"

"One new Winchester and ammunition," Cal finally said with gut wrenching reluctance. It didn't matter, whiskey or guns, both were illegal as hell to trade to known hostiles. If the Army ever learned of such a transaction, he'd be in deep trouble—but the Army had never got Teddy Swain back either. He looked at the stone face in front of him.

"Whiskey, cartridges, rifle. That's all I've got. Can I make a trade with them?"

Billy shrugged. "Most of the *broncos* are in Mexico."

"Is the boy down there?" Cal demanded.

"Maybe, maybe not. You got whiskey and rifle, we go see."

A week later, Cal arrived in Tucson, dismounted heavily. Forced to grasp the saddle horn for several minutes to let his aching legs become sea worthy. Bone weary, he swayed as he crossed her porch to knock on the door. When she opened the door, her eyes flew open in shock. Her face paled when she looked beyond him at the other horse and rider. Finally she managed a shriek at her discovery.

"You found my boy! Teddy!" She rushed past Cal to hug the quiet boy who slipped from his horse.

"Teddy! Teddy! Are you all right?" she asked, her hands touching his dust-streaked face, searching him for wounds and imperfections.

"I'm fine, mother," he said, sounding embarrassed by her attention.

The boy would be better in time. The shock would wear off, Cal felt certain. Teddy Swain had been through a lot and he'd seen more than most grownups would in a lifetime.

She turned with her eyes filled with tears that she couldn't control. "How can I ever repay you, Mr. Jones?"

"Well, ma'am, I reckon fifty bucks would be enough. But I have to warn you that I lost your rifle." He shook his head to silence the boy's protest.

"A rifle? Who cares about a rifle?" She almost laughed aloud at his concern as she wiped at the tears on her cheeks.

"Well ma'am, lets not talk about it ever again then?"

"Certainly, Mr. Jones. I shall consider the matter settled."

Fine, he didn't figure the boy would mention it either and perhaps the Army would never learn he had traded a new .44/40 and whiskey to some hostile Apaches for the ransom payment. It would just as well be left unsaid.

She paused in the doorway on her way to get his pay and looked back in disbelief at Cal and her son..

"Won't you consider moving in with Teddy and me? We have this large house—"

Cal shook his head. "I learned a lot of things out there." He motioned to the distant mountains. "Lately, I've wondered why I drank so much. Now I know, my scouting days are over. Ain't nothing left for me to do, but three things."

"Oh? What's that?"

"Get drunk, being drunk and getting that way again." He waved off her protest. "Don't worry about me, ma'am. You've got a fine boy here to raise. He's plenty tough and he'll make a good man. The Apaches thought so too." If they hadn't, the boy would not be alive.

Cal and Teddy shook hands while she went indoors. Neither spoke but their nods were enough. Then the boy went inside the house.

"Mr. Jones," Colleen said rushing out side, "Here is a hundred dollars and it is not enough for all you have done. Take that horse too."

"No ma'am, I have no place to keep him. Besides I've got no reason to own one."

Unable to contain herself, she took him in a surprise hug and kissed him several times on the cheek. Wet kisses, for she had let the tears run down unheeded since he had arrived with the boy. "You ever need something, anything, money—for your whiskey, whatever, you come see me?"

His face afire with embarrassment, he could only mumble thanks and close his fist on the money she gave him. He stepped back. Then he remembered Gladys. She'd like all the whiskey he could afford to buy with this money. Of course, when the word got out he'd brought the boy back, they'd buy him several rounds of drinks in all the bars. But after the notoriety wore off, he'd have to go back to swamping out saloons again.

He looked forward to the whiskey that he intended to drink, it would make him forget, forget growing old and the sad state of his blood brothers, the wild Apache. His tongue was so thick for need of a drink, he doubted he could even talk as he hurried to find Gladys and share the good news.

Old Man Clanton's Last Fandango

Her cuss words in Spanish exploded in the empty bar room. He raised up in the side booth from his mescal induced siesta. What had *her majesty* so upset this time?

He scrubbed his beard stubbled mouth on his calloused palm. By then, she came whirling up beside him. Her red skirt twisting from side to side, she halted like a trained horse on her heels before him. The fury written on her honey colored face forced him to sit up, lest in her impatience she struck him.

"What's wrong?"

"Stupid donkey!" Hands planted on her shapely hips, her dark eyes shot darts of anger like a stone grind wheel making a shower of sparks sharpening a steel blade. Her exposed cleavage that showed in the open necked blouse quaked with her upset. Even wound up in her anger, her beauty made him feel strongly attached to her.

"Who?" His eyes narrowed in serious consideration.

"Don Pentales."

"What the hell did he do to put you in such a vise?" Damn. Enough was enough. Whatever had her so on fire needed to be brought out in the open.

"You know he was supposed to bring a beef for me to butcher."

"He said he had a fat three-year-old steer for your barbecue—" He stopped.

Someone parted the bat wing doors and pushed his way inside the dimly lit cantina. She turned and looked hard at the great Chihuahua peaked sombrero. Under his tailored short waist coat, he had on a snowy, ruffled front shirt, This fancy hombre wore fine chaps, two six-guns on his narrow hips and the great silver rowels strapped on his boot heels rang like bells. He cast a look sideways at her, then at him.

"You are open?" he asked in Castilian Spanish.

"*Si, señor*," she said and wadded her skirt in her hand and hurried to get behind the bar to serve him. While she went, the stranger keep a cold gaze on him for longer than would be considered friendly. An appraising stare by one who obviously knew no fear. Her latest customer might be a *bustamente*, a *pistolero* or even some apparition that came out of the Sierra Madras like smoke on the wind.

"Could I buy you a drink?" the man asked and nodded cordially with his invitation.

"Yes. I would drink with you." His tongue thick enough by this time from the nap, something needed to cut through the depth.

"Good. To drink alone is like playing with yourself. There are better ways." A smile parted his thin lips and even in the dark room, his straight teeth shown like polished pearls.

"What brings a man like you to Azipe?" he asked.

"Me?" The look of innocence on his handsome face meant nothing. "

This town has few things a man of your obvious means would need."

"Ah, there you are wrong, my *amigo*."

Regardless of what the stranger said to deny it, if he came to find either fame or fortune in this dingy place of cockroaches and ugly putas, he would be disappointed. Even the chickens about this village laid runny eggs. The skinny cows gave blue john from their cheesy bags and the burros birthed crook legged offspring.

"Have you heard of a man called Clanton?"

"Who has not heard of that butcher." He took the glass of brown mescal and toasted the buyer.

With his thumb, the stranger raised the great sombrero and nodded. "Then you know where he lives?"

"Not many miles from here."

"*Bueno, señor.*"

"What plans have you for Old Man Clanton? Sell him cattle? They say he has all the business with the Indian agencies, the U.S. Army. You want to sell beef to any of them you must first pay the old man."

"Him and those *bastardos* in Tucson." The voice sounded harsher. His words this time snapped like the braided cotton popper on the end of a six-foot bullwhip.

"You mean—" He looked around to be certain they were alone and no one could hear him. "The Tucson Ring?"

"Exactly." The intruder looked at the glass, then he took another deep drink. "They sell the Apaches guns and sell the army horses, food, and blankets. They keep the Indian agencies warehouses full of wormy bacon and flour that's half chaff. And they get paid for it as prime stuff."

"But that is beyond the border."

"There is no border for Old Man Clanton. He kills, robs and rustles in Sonora. Then he sells it for American pesos. What does the border mean to such a weasel?"

"A convenience."

"Ah, *si*. Have some more mescal, *amigo*." He refilled both their glasses and nodded to affirm his words.

Somehow he began to realize that this stranger represented a profit for him He did not know how, but he became more confident of his discovery by the minute. This fancy dressed rooster could be quite a valuable acquaintance in his circle of friends. It was not the strong drink they bathed their throats with that made his mind wander into rooms where there were gold bars stacked. He had not felt even a small buzz like a fly from the liquor, but the stranger's words built castles for him in the great clouds that gathered across the skies in July.

"They say you are a powder monkey."

He nodded. "I can blow a mountain range flat if you have enough or I can crack a seam in a granite mountain so narrow a paper won't fit between it."

The man nodded as if he had heard of such deeds and was satisfied. "Now I want you to work for me."

"You have spoken of two things so far." At ease with this fine dressed one, he put his elbows on the bar and considered his own grizzled face in the mirror behind the bar. The white sprouts on his face. The frost above his ears in the thin dark hair. No longer a young man who could take on three putas a night and make each one at long last beg for him to quit. Still he was not old, except his left ear had a constant ring in it from a too close blast. That fuse had burned too fast.

The stranger joined him. Shoulder to shoulder, their elbows resting on the edge, drinking her best mescal and making plans. It was like days gone by, when he feasted at great tables with patrons and spoke of opening mines to expose the gold secreted in the mountains' vaginas. He felt the swell of his youth returning.

He looked over at him. "What rocks do you need split asunder?"

The man put down his glass and leaned on his right elbow. "I want old man Clanton and his gang blown to hell and gone."

He knew the man's true purpose at last. To this, he closed his right eye and considered the matter. He had blown up train bridges for various reasons. Once, he failed and that was why he resided in Sonora. But to blow up a person—who was old man Clanton anyway? A killer of innocent woman and children, a rustler who stole the poor rancher's stock and shot them if they complained. Why would he lose any sleep over such a thing?

Not just anytime," the stranger said.

"Not just anytime?" He looked pained at the well-dressed man beside him; he even felt a little jealous over his ownership of the snowy, ruffled shirt.

"We must do it when he and all his gang are inside the casa."

"But how will we do it then?"

"You know Generale Crook?"

"I've heard of him. But I never met him."

"He is a smart man, he hires Apaches to find Apaches."

"The scouts. Tom Horn rides with them. I know him"

"Yes. An Apache can walk through your room at night and steal you blind and you would never know it."

"But I'm not an Apache." He pointed at his chest with his index finger.

"I will get you three of them. They can plant the charges for you. Do you see my plan?"

"I do. But isn't he well guarded? I mean he has armed men and mean dogs that bark. I heard he was tougher than Fort Bowie to get close to."

From his jacket pocket, the stranger produced a ring. Gold band with rubies. Even in the dim light it shown.

"What is that for?"

"That ring was on the old man's night stand beside his bed. It was stolen off Señora Antonette Maria Consuela Reales when they raided the Reales hacienda. One of your Apaches went inside the Clanton's casa four nights ago and took that ring."

He nodded. Impressed.

"They cut her finger off for this ring."

A shiver of cold ran up his spine despite the hot bar room.

"Saturday night, the gang will be there. Both his sons. Spawn of the devil and all his banditos."

"I'll need supplies."

"They are waiting on pack mules, not a hundred yards from this cantina."

"Fuses, detonators, matches, waxed cord," he reeled off the things he could think of.

"They are all here."

"The Apaches?"

"They will be there when we need them."

Trapped. He felt that this man would take nothing from him , but 'I-will-go-with-you.'

Then from inside his fine coat, he took out two pouches that clunked heavy on the counter.

"Two thousand in gold coins."

Sparkling new, the yellow buckskin sacks gleamed on the wash worn wood. For a moment, he dared not to touch them. The words, pieces-of-eight crossed his mind. Then at last, he shoved them toward the back of the bar and his gaze met hers. The paleness in her complexion made the circles under her eyes look like rings of charcoal. For once, this firecracker made no loud explosion. She stood behind the bar and fizzled in some depleting form. He gave a wave of his hand for her to put them away. Then with a dull nod, she took one in each hand and dropped to her knees to place them in the small safe beneath the bar.

"Get me some things," he said to her and she obediently rushed off. She knew what he meant. A towel, soap, a change of underwear, a shirt. Some tobacco, papers. He'd add a few bottles of the good stuff to his tucker.

Damn, how long since he had had an adventure? The strength began to grown inside him. Only this job he could never brag about. Not like the time he opened the great silver vein in Los Gados Mine. Or when he found the streak of gold they'd lost—she piled his sack on the bar.

"*Dos mescal*," he said and smiled at her.

She nodded. The ghostly pallor still on her face; he felt a twinge of guilt. The bottles wrapped in cloth stowed in his bag, he picked it up and nodded to his new amigo.

"I'm ready."

"*Vaya con el dios*," she whispered and crossed herself.

He reached over the bar, swept her up against it and kissed her hard on the lips. "Sleep well, my love, I will return in a few days. We can do what we want then, no?"

"Yes," she whispered like the wind in the cottonwoods.

So he rode a fine gray gelding beside the stranger's dancing horse, the fiery color of polished copper. The steed's blood boiled with the pedigree of a king's stable. The purest of lineage, the fleetest of the desert Moor's great breeding.

They said the Mohammeden conquest gave Spain the spiral turrets on their buildings. But besides the long horned cattle, they left behind strains of their equine stock that knew no equal for endurance and speed. And as he rode beside this knight, he began recalling his own days of youth spent in Madrid at the bullfights. Of women he toasted, loved and the hot winds on the plains. He raised his hat and wiped the gritty sweat on his shirtsleeve. The same flames of hell toasted this land of greasewood as it did the Iberian Peninsula.

The Apaches weren't there one minute, then like mirages out of the heat waves, they appeared, riding short legged horses, tough as mesquite wood. They came in spotted colors. Those stiff trotting ponies. An affection for such coats afflicted the aborigines across the land. It was not only an Apache trait, but rather all such men of the red race coveted the paints and piebald.

In his mind as he rode, he planned the length of each fuse. The size of the charges. No need to be stingy, the many boxes of explosives aboard the mules could flatten a mountain range if properly planted. His operation would be to send the Apaches inside with enough dynamite, fused and ready for them to light it and still be time for them to get outside before it went off. There could be no mistakes.

If anyone in the house discovered the lighted sticks they could rush outside and perhaps miss being blown up. So care in planting them would be everything.

"Yes, they will put them out of sight," the one on the copper horse assured him.

The next day was spent in an oven hot canyon, wrapping the sticks in bundles with waxed string. The ends of the dynamite pried open and the blasting caps inserted. Fuse stuck in them after he carefully burned lengths and used his pocket watch to learn the time necessary to consume the footage.

He showed the pan-faced Apaches the consumption of the fuses. They nodded in approval.

Then came the sunset. A fiery ball that sunk slower than usual. This may have been the longest day in his life. He could recall none this long before. Charges ready.

His messengers of death spent the day, squatted in their loin cloths, smoked cigarettes and were unmoved by either the pesky flies or the oppressive heat. At last, darkness veiled the land.

"I thought all Apaches dreaded the night?"

"Only dying during the night disturbs them," his employer said. Then he went over and spoke to his Apaches in guttural words and they went for their ponies. The five of them rode out on the grease wood flats and in the distance they could make out the yellow lights of the Clanton House. He could even turn his good ear and hear music and laughter.

Fandango going on. They must have scored a big one. The Apaches dismounted and squatted. In the starlight, he was uncertain if they were a few yards from him or if they were ghosts. Somewhere a coyote called and another answered.

The one in charge drew out a brass telescope and looked across the plains. He handed it to him to use. Through the eye piece, he could see a half naked woman being pursued by two men on the porch. One wore no pants.

Their party must be wild. Then he turned at the soft shuffle of more horses coming.

"No worry. They are with us."

He could see they were armed with new Winchesters when they drew up, staying apart from him, the stranger and the Apaches. Their faces hidden in night by the shade of their hats. No one smoked. No one talked. Only sounds were the creaks of their saddle leather, or an occasional snort of a horse.

He did not dwell long on who they were. They were his backup, he decided. If the charges failed to eliminate any of the clan, then they would do the job.

He kept time by the big dipper. Past midnight, the sounds from the far away party grew muted. The man waved his Apaches toward the house. Each one was armed with a gunnysack, full of charges; they soon evaporated into the silvery night.

Then the organizer gave instructions for the gun bearers to surround the place and sent them off in pairs. The two of them were alone with the horses.

"Him and his kind deserve no mercy," he said and handed a bottle to him.

He shook his head. He had no need for a drink. He might never drink again. The dipper stopped its movement. Perhaps the earth too had stopped spinning on its axis. Only the night bugs buzzed. No Apaches, no riflemen.

If a great bear had vomited up fire, then that would best describe the multi explosions that send shock waves across the open ground at them. High in the sky projectiles shot in an eerie red-orange light. The night held fearsome screams. Then a few rifle shots. Not many, but they reverberated across the flats and echoes answered.

"*Mia amigo, gracia* for your time and expert work. If I ever need you again. I will send word. The gray horse is your bonus for a job well done."

Alone, he rode back to Azipe. By mid morning, when he reined up before the cantina, his eyes felt like sand pits and his spine seemed deformed from the long hours in the saddle. He spotted the boy of ten.

"Take my grand *caballo*. Water him slowly, rub him down and feed him soft hay."

"*Ah, si, Señor Gringo*. I am good with horses."

"I know that is why I chose you." He dismounted slowly and let his sea legs take form before he released the saddle horn. Then his gaze stopped on the faded green bat wing doors; he hobbled for the cantina's sanctuary. Anxious to see her again.

She rushed from behind the bar. Her arms flew around him.

"You're all right. You're fine."

"Sure." He set the bag on the table and the bottles clunked.

She frowned. "You never drank the mescal?"

He looked up at the dusty buffalo head above the bar and shook his head. "I may never drink again," he said aloud.

What was a stuffed bison head doing in Mexico anyway? What was he doing there? He rocked her in his arms to savor her ripe body against his.

"Have you ever been to Texas?" he asked her, kissing her sweet smelling hair and ear.

"No. Why?"

"Let's sell this place. Get a casa along the Guadalupe River. I can catch catfish. You can grow a garden."

"Why?"

"'Cause I belong there. With you."

"If you say so, my darling, we will go there."

"Good, now I must sleep."

Twenty years later, he sat in the warm sun before the jackal. The rays felt good. The young reporter from the San Antonio Herald was asking questions and taking notes.

"Ah, Señor Kelly, did you ever know any big bandits on the border in those days?"

"I heard of one."

"Who was that, señor?"

"Old Man Clanton."

"You saw him?"

"Yes, I saw him go to hell one night."

"That must have been something exciting, señor. Can you tell me more."

He shook his head. "No, it's my siesta time. But believe me, he really went there."

$$\ominus \ \ominus \ \ominus$$

Author's note: Historical legend blamed Old Man Clanton and his gang for the brutal robbery of a Mexican gold mule train in Skeleton Canyon. The story goes that a single survivor of that massacre, a boy, grew up, became wealthy and led a well planned raid on Clanton's Hacienda, which leveled the place to the ground. Neither the old man nor any of his gang members present survived the raid.

Luckily, Ike Clanton and some his siblings were in Tombstone that evening harassing the Earps and Doc Holiday. Later on, after trying all day to pick a fight with the Earps, Ike chickened out at the OK Corral gunfight—he fled into Fly's Studio, screaming, "Don't shoot me! I'm unarmed."

Ike and the others killed in the famous incident were held up as model citizens by Tombstone's Anti-Earp forces in the stormy days after the shootout. Six months later, Ike was shot and killed by a guard while he attempted to hold up a stagecoach, being the good citizen he was.

Dusty Richards

Dusty is a professional rodeo announcer, auctioneer, and cattleman. He serves on the local rodeo board, rural electric coop board, several writers organizations, including the Ozark Creative Writers Conference in Eureka Springs, Arkansas. He is a past board member of the Western Writers of America and headed their constitutional changes. He also co-announces the National Chuckwagon Races and the Texas National Chuckwagon Races.

CPSIA information can be obtained at www.ICGtesting.com
Printed in the USA
LVOW06s1025110514

385295LV00001B/201/P

9 780970 750792